BOSS ROMANCE

VICTORIA QUINN

CONTENTS

Hartwick Publishing

Boss Romance

Copyright © 2018 by Victoria Quinn

1

TITAN

THORN'S MOTHER called me again.

I never listened to her voice mail, so I didn't have a clue what she said. She must be furious with me, even if it seemed like Thorn was the one who left. Avoiding conflict wasn't in my nature since I always met my challenges head on. This wasn't me at all. On top of that, I respected Liv. She'd been like a mother to me. I didn't want to cut her out like this, not give her an explanation when she deserved one.

Without knowing what to expect, I answered, "Hey, Liv."

"Titan?" Her emotion was at an all-time high. She wasn't in tears, but she was audibly distressed. "I called you a week ago."

"I'm sorry I didn't call you back." I didn't make an

excuse for avoiding her. I was obviously deflecting her, and we both knew that.

"I don't understand what's going on. Last time I saw the two of you, everything seemed fine. And then I hear this story on the news...that Thorn left you for some ho. I don't understand..."

"Have you spoken to Thorn?"

"He won't take my calls."

I knew he was avoiding her because he didn't want to listen to her disappointment. He was definitely a mama's boy. Always had been. It was one of the reasons why I loved him. He treated his mother so well, but he also put his foot down when she crossed a line. He managed to establish his space in a respectful way. "It's been hard for both of us. He just needs some space right now. He'll call you when he's ready to talk."

"Titan, help me understand. Why would my son do this to you?"

I gripped the armrest of my chair and felt the flood of guilt drown me. This was entirely my fault. Liv thought her son was an asshole, when it was completely untrue. How could I let her continue to think that? "It's more complicated than that. I know Thorn looks like the bad guy in this, but he's not."

"It sure seems that way. And I raised my son better than this."

Another bomb of guilt. "Liv, you raised the best son in the world."

"How can you speak so highly of him after he dumped you like that?"

I wanted to tell her the truth, but I knew Thorn didn't want that. "We had more problems than met the eye. Don't judge Thorn for what's happened. I'm responsible for a lot of issues. I don't want you to think less of him when he doesn't deserve it."

"But you're like a daughter to me, Titan..."

I didn't expect the tears to well in my eyes so quickly. I had a soft spot for his family, always had. They'd made me feel welcome when I was alone in the world. They'd made every holiday feel special. They'd made me a member of their family from the moment they met me. "You've been like a mother to me, Liv. But please give Thorn the benefit of the doubt. I love him very much. Always have and always will."

I STRUGGLED WITH MY DECISION ALL DAY. I WENT BACK and forth, growing scared and then chickening out again. I wanted to call Thorn, but I suspected he wouldn't answer. He would reject me like he promised he would.

I couldn't face that heartbreak.

So I texted him. *Your mother called me a few times. I couldn't avoid her forever, so I answered. She's upset about the breakup, but I told her I was responsible, without giving any details. You should call her.*

As I expected, he didn't text back. I was used to seeing those three dots light up immediately once I contacted him. He used to be readily available at all times. It didn't matter what he was doing, he always made time for me. He could be in the biggest meeting of his career, but that didn't matter to him—not when it came to me.

The dots never showed up.

And now I missed them more than ever.

———

JESSICA'S VOICE SHATTERED MY THOUGHTS. "TITAN, I have Mr. Vincent Hunt on the line for you."

Now when I heard his name, I didn't tense in dread. I didn't prepare myself for a threat or something worse. With every private conversation I had with him, I saw a new side to his character. He was a ruthless shark in a business world, but in my eyes, he was just a father who struggled with parenting. "Thank you, Jessica. Patch him through."

The light turned on, and I took the call. "Hello, Mr. Hunt. How can I help you?"

"Please call me Vincent."

I didn't know anyone else who was on a first-name basis with him. It made me feel special when I shouldn't. "Of course. How are you?"

"Hungry. Will you have lunch with me?"

I hadn't expected anything specific when he called, but I certainly didn't expect an invitation like that. I didn't have an answer because I still didn't understand the request. As much as I wanted to ask why he wanted to see me, I didn't want to be rude.

Vincent must have read my mood. "No tricks. Just want to get to know you a little better. You're the one who said you'll be my daughter-in-law someday."

I did say that.

"I have a table at Dorian's. Will I see you there in fifteen minutes?"

I felt deceitful meeting Diesel's father without telling him, but I wasn't hiding anything either. If Diesel asked about it, I would tell him. "I'll see you there."

THE HOSTESS MUST HAVE BEEN EXPECTING ME BECAUSE she greeted me before I even completely stepped through the doors. "Mr. Hunt is waiting for you." She walked in front of me and guided me to the private table he had in the rear of the restaurant. It wasn't close to other guests, allowing for a private conversation in confidence.

He had the same aura as his son. He was hard and calloused, a muscular man with the fitness of a horse. Like a fine wine, he'd aged well. He still possessed obvious charm, handsomeness, and clear sex appeal. Whenever I saw him with a woman in her twenties, it didn't surprise me at all. Vincent Hunt got as much tail as his son.

He watched me with the same coffee-colored eyes, sitting with square shoulders and a straight back. He rose from his chair with elegance before he greeted me. Instead of kissing me on the cheek like Thorn did, he shook my hand.

I thought it was appropriate.

"It's nice to see you." He gripped my hand with obvious strength, the veins on the surface of his hands looking like prominent webs. He didn't give me a smile, but his dark eyes seemed gentler now that he was looking at me.

"You too."

He maneuvered behind me and pulled out my chair for me.

Didn't expect that. "Thank you..." I didn't need a man to pull out my chair for me, especially during a business meeting. But I knew this didn't exactly fit into that category. I took the action as a compliment, that he was treating me like a lady rather than a rival executive.

He sat down again and took a sip of his wine.

It was the first time I'd interacted with Vincent Hunt out of the office. Even in a change of scenery, he still seemed as threatening. He had a hard jaw like his son, piercing eyes, and a set of shoulders that would make professional fighters uneasy.

Diesel might hate his father, but they were so much alike.

"Do you like wine?" he asked.

"I do."

"Red or white?"

"Both."

He gave a slight smile. "You have good taste."

The waiter arrived at our table and took my drink order.

I ordered an Old Fashioned instead. While he was there, we also ordered our meals. I had a salad, and Vincent ordered chicken breast with greens. The waiter disappeared, taking the menus with him.

Vincent kept his hand on his glass as he watched me, the same unblinking stare that Diesel wore all the time. "Is that your drink?"

"Usually."

"Excellent choice."

"I've been trying to cut back. It's been getting easier." I had no idea why I told him that. It was unnecessary information, one of my truths that didn't put me in a good light. But then again, it didn't matter whether Vincent Hunt liked me or not. I didn't care about his opinion.

"May I ask why?"

"Diesel said I drank too much."

"And do you agree?"

I nodded.

He swirled his wine before he took another drink. "I've used it as a crutch as well. Most people have."

Instead of judging me, he shared his two cents. That was unexpected.

"What's Diesel's drink?"

"He has a few. Scotch on the rocks with a twist.

Red wine. And he's become a fan of Old Fashioneds since he met me."

He nodded. "He and I have similar tastes."

The waiter returned with my drink and set it beside me. It was only noon and far too early to drink at this intensity, but I was having a serious lunch and I could use something good to calm the nerves.

Vincent returned to staring at me. He had no problem looking at people directly, even if it made them uncomfortable.

I was the same way, so it didn't bother me one bit. "Tell me about yourself," he said.

"What do you want to know?"

"Anything you're comfortable sharing with me."

I drank from my glass as I watched him. "Will you tell me things about yourself?" I'd rather have an open dialogue than an interrogation.

"Of course. If you're interested, that is."

"Why wouldn't I be?"

He drank from his glass again. "Despite what people may think, I'm not that interesting."

"I'm not either."

"I don't agree with that. Even before I knew Diesel was fascinated with you, I respected you. You handle business with grace. Even when the competition is sexist and jealous, you don't let it get to you. You work ten times as hard to reap the same rewards. You're a woman who turned a few pennies into billions. As the richest woman in the world, you're definitely interesting. It's very difficult to impress me, but, Ms. Titan, but I'm very impressed by you."

I kept a straight face even though his words touched me. Not all successful men complimented my achievements. Sometimes they questioned them, assuming there was a man standing behind me in the shadows. Sometimes people attributed my success to luck. And worst of all, some people thought I slept my way to the top. "Thank you."

"You're most welcome," he said. "I didn't have any daughters, but I imagine if I had, they would be just like you."

Another compliment.

"My son has made a lot of stupid choices. You're definitely not one of them." He brought the glass to his lips and took a drink while he kept his eyes on me. He studied me like a painting in a gallery, examining all the subtle features that couldn't be spotted right away. You had to be patient before the nuances became apparent. "You were close with your father?" he asked.

"Very. He was all I had."

"Would you mind telling me about him?" He shifted his position in his chair and came closer to the table, giving me even more attention than before.

"He was a painter. So he was always chasing jobs. The winters were always hard. The summers were difficult because I hardly saw him. He was the hardest working person I ever knew."

His eyes remained trained on me, hanging on to every word.

"He was a poet as well. Sometimes he wrote short stories. His dream was to be a published writer. He said he would be rich one day and make all our problems go away. But then he was diagnosed with cancer...and he died shortly afterward."

Vincent's expression didn't change, but his shoulders stiffened.

"I bought a publishing house just so I could publish his poems. The sales aren't amazing, but we sell a few copies every day. The business is dying because it's becoming obsolete. Keeping it isn't profitable at all. In fact, I lose more money every year. But I'd rather make his dream a reality—even if he isn't here to see it."

It was the first time Vincent dropped his gaze that afternoon. He looked at his glass before he took a long drink. Then he refilled it from the bottle sitting there. Perhaps the intimacy was too much. Perhaps the heartbreak was obvious on my face. He stared at the glass for another moment before he looked at me. "I'm sorry. I know that doesn't change anything. I'm sure it doesn't mean anything to you... but I'm sorry."

I heard the sincerity in his tone and saw the same emotion in his eyes. "I know you are."

"When I lost my wife..." His eyes drifted away, and he shook his head slightly. "I never really got over it. I think about her every day. Every morning, I wake up alone and wish she were still beside me."

Anytime I spoke about my father, it was with heartbreak. But hearing Vincent speak of his wife made my heart break in a different way.

"I understand how you feel, Titan. Just want you to know that."

My fingers wrapped around my glass, but I didn't take a drink. I let the silence stretch on between us, growing bigger and deeper. We both thought about the ones we loved, those we lost far too soon. "That was how I met your son. He wanted to buy the publishing house from me, but I refused to sell."

The corner of his mouth rose in a smile. "I'm sure he didn't like that."

"No."

"And I'm sure he didn't stop until he got what he wanted."

"You're right. But I never sold it to him."

"And I'm sure that's the moment he fell in love with you."

A soft smile came over my lips. "I'm not sure when it happened, honestly."

"How long has it been?"

I counted back to the first time we met. "About seven months."

"You kept it a secret for a pretty long time, then."

"Yeah, we did."

He rested one hand on the table, his high-end watch reflecting the lights from the ceiling. "May I ask why you were publicly involved with Thorn?"

"I already answered that question."

"You said it was a business relationship. But that doesn't explain why you wanted to marry someone for convenience instead of love. I'm very biased, but I would choose love every single time."

Just like Diesel, he had a soft spot deep inside his chest, a side he never let anyone see. "I'm sure you heard that story about my abusive relationship..."

He nodded. "But I don't see what that has to do with anything."

"I gave up on love after that. I gave my heart to someone who didn't deserve it, and as a result, I vowed never to put myself in that situation again. Love was something I never felt after that, so marrying Thorn didn't seem like a sacrifice. But when I met Diesel...everything became complicated."

"I'm glad Diesel changed your mind. There are a lot of scumbags out there, men who shouldn't be allowed to call themselves men. But there are a lot of great men who would do anything for the woman they love. They'd rather die than let a single tear fall down her cheek. When we've been hurt, the hardest thing to do is trust again. But once we do, we realize there's much more good than there is bad."

I smiled, touched by his optimism. He seemed too intense to feel anything positive.

"My son and I have disagreed about a lot of things, but I raised him better than that. You never have to worry about that with him."

"I know. He's a good man."

"Thank you," he said quietly. "I'm actually quite proud of him...even though I've never told him."

I wished Diesel could hear this himself. I could relay the message, but it wouldn't be the same coming from me. "You should."

His eyes shifted away, taking in the rest of the restaurant. "He doesn't care, Titan. And I don't blame him."

"He does."

"You must have told him about our last conversation. What was his response?" He looked back at me.

"To be honest, he was pretty quiet."

Vincent couldn't hide the disappointment in his gaze.

"But I think it meant something to him. I think we just have a lot of work to do. Even if the sentiment is there, there's so much damage that it can't be fixed overnight. But I truly believe there is hope."

"I'm not so sure," he said with a sigh.

"How about you ask him to lunch instead of me?"

"And you think he'd show up?" he countered.

No. "Probably not. But if you ask a few times, he'll eventually say yes."

Vincent sighed in disagreement.

"You need to start with Brett first. Make things right, and then Diesel will let his guard down."

"Like I said, Brett doesn't need me. I can promise you he has no interest in a relationship with me. I've never been a father to him."

"He doesn't have a mother or a father," I reminded him. "You're all he has."

He tapped his fingers against the surface of the wood as he continued to look around the restaurant.

"What happened with Brett?"

"I'm sure Diesel already told you."

"I want your version. You seem like a compassionate man. Why were you so cold to Brett?"

"My version is his version." He turned his gaze back to me, looking hostile. "I did everything he's accused me of. I didn't treat Brett the same way I treated my own sons. And I never considered him to be a son."

His harshness surprised me, especially after all the heartfelt things he'd said. "Why?"

He drank his wine again, taking so long it didn't seem like he was going to answer me at all. He finally set the glass down and licked his lips. "Every time I look at Brett...I'm reminded that my wife loved someone else before me. After she was gone, I saw her face in him every single day...but I didn't see myself. It pained me to know she had spent time with someone else, that we could have had more time together if we'd met sooner. I never overcame my jealousy. It never had anything to do with Brett... and I treated him badly because of it. It was wrong of me, and I won't make excuses for it. I know my wife is in heaven because she was the most compassionate woman that ever lived...and she'll never forgive me for what I did."

His explanation wasn't a justification of his actions. But at least it made sense. "You can't take back what you did, but you can change things. Talk to Brett. Start a new relationship."

"Like I said, he doesn't want anything to do with me."

"How do you know unless you try?"

He shook his head. "We don't have a connection. We have nothing in common. He's older than my sons. He doesn't need me for anything. He has his own life now. He's a very successful man, so he's doing just fine."

"You loved his mother, and he loved her. You have a pretty profound connection."

He didn't argue with that.

"I think you should try, Vincent. I can help. But the question is...do you still want nothing to do with him?" Whatever his answer might be, I still wanted to help him heal his relationship with Diesel. But I needed to know exactly what I was dealing with.

He stared at his wine for a long time before he answered. "I do. I want to make things right for my wife...to make sure her son has family. And I would like to get to know him. How can I not care about someone who has my wife's eyes?"

My hands loosened on my glass as the relief flooded through. "I'll talk to Brett and get him to have lunch with us."

"He'll say no, Titan."

"Then if I have to trick him, I will."

He wore a sarcastic smile. "I'm sure that will go over well."

I had to bring these men back together. I had to give Diesel something he didn't realize he needed. I knew his battered relationship with his father haunted him. When he turned angry and aggressive, I knew it bothered him down to his core. Those feelings of rage only remained because he had unresolved issues.

"Thank you for helping me, Titan. Your time is valuable, but you're spending it on me."

I smiled. "There's nowhere else I'd rather be."

2

HUNT

AFTER I WENT to the gym, I usually headed home to shower.

But now, I went straight to Titan's penthouse.

We'd never had a discussion about where we would be staying. Her place wasn't necessarily bigger or better than mine, but since she called it home, I went wherever she was. I walked inside her penthouse in my workout clothes with my suit in my duffel bag. She had an employee collect her dry cleaning every night, so I added it to the pile to be picked up. "Baby, I'm here."

She walked out of the kitchen in her work clothes, a black apron tied around her waist.

I nearly did a double take. "What's this?"

"An apron." She rose on her tiptoes since her

heels were gone and kissed me on the lips. "People use them when they cook."

I grabbed her ass through her skirt as I kissed her. "I know what it is. You just don't strike me as the kind of woman who wears one."

"I don't want to get anything on my expensive blouse."

"Then maybe you should cook with nothing on..." I kept kissing her, my eyes on hers as I squeezed her gorgeous behind.

"Ouch. That would hurt."

"Then how about just the apron?"

"I guess I could give that a try." She gave me one more kiss before she settled back on her flat feet. "How was your day?"

"Good. Yours?"

She hesitated slightly before she answered. "Good. Dinner will be ready by the time you're out of the shower." She started to drift away.

I grabbed her by the wrist and tugged her back to me. "As much as I appreciate a hot meal every night when I come home, you don't need to cook for me." She could always hire someone to do that for her, but she was an extremely private person who hardly let anyone into her domain.

"I know. I do it because I enjoy it."

That was a sweet answer—and sexy. "I can always whip up something if you need a break."

"Will you cook naked?" she teased.

I smiled before I rubbed my nose against hers. "Sure."

"Ooh..." She walked away and headed back into the kitchen, shaking her gorgeous ass as she walked.

I stared until she was completely gone from sight —a hard dick in my shorts.

WE SAT ACROSS FROM EACH OTHER, BOTH OF US enjoying a glass of wine with dinner. I'd never cooked for a woman before or had her cook for me. It was just sex, sometimes dinner and drinks, and that was about it.

But now we did this on a nightly basis.

It was boring, quiet, predictable...I loved it.

She drank her wine in between bites, sticking to one glass without refilling it. She'd taken my words to heart and watched her alcohol intake. I never considered her to be an alcoholic, but I didn't want her to overdo it either. She could handle her liquor better than anyone I'd ever met, which was why it concerned me more. Before she even realized it, she would have more to drink on a Tuesday than a man on a Friday night in a bar.

"I think you should come back to Stratosphere." She held her fork in her hand as she gazed at me across the table. "I know you walked away because of me...and it hasn't been the same since you left."

I hadn't wanted to leave the company either. I'd only done it because I didn't have a choice. Now that we'd worked things out, it didn't make sense for me to stay away. "I'd love to come back if you'll have me. I enjoyed working with you."

"Great." She smiled in relief, as if she'd expected me to give a different answer. "I guess we'll get the legal teams together again."

"They get paid either way, so they won't care."

"Yeah, I guess not." She turned her attention back to her food and pushed it around with a fork.

I watched the way a few strands of hair fell in front of her face. She was beautiful without even trying, a work of art. There was a distinct sadness that accompanied her features constantly now. I knew it was because of Thorn, and I always steered clear of any subject that could be related to him. I still believed I could bring them back together; I just wasn't sure how. But I would find a way. "Anything interesting happen today?"

She was about to take a break but chose to put her fork down instead. "Actually, yeah."

"What?" I took a bite and chewed as I stared at her. She was still in her work clothes, but the apron was gone. Once I'd showered, I'd pulled on a pair of sweatpants and nothing else, making myself comfortable in her home. She liked my choice of attire anyway.

When she paused before she answered, I knew what she had to say was significant. "I had lunch with your father."

Vincent Hunt seemed to be the subject of most of our conversations lately. "Where did you bump into him?"

"Actually, he called me and invited me to lunch."

Even if my father was no longer hostile, I didn't trust him. Dinner was forgotten and the paranoia sunk in. "What did he want? Did he threaten you?"

She chuckled like the suggestion was absolutely absurd. "No."

But it wasn't absurd. My father had manipulated me my entire life. Just in the last few months, he'd been intent on destroying my life. It wasn't a ridiculous suggestion to make, and I didn't want Titan to forget that.

"He said he wanted to get to know me."

Both of my eyebrows nearly lurched off my face. "Did he come on to you?"

This time, she rolled her eyes. "Diesel, come on."

"Did he?" I pressed.

"Your father has never looked at me like that. And trust me, I can tell."

My father's dates were always in their twenties, younger than both Titan and me. He clearly had a preference for the young and the beautiful. Titan fit that criteria perfectly, but she also had so many more features that made her innately desirable.

"When I spoke to him in his office, I told him I would be his daughter-in-law someday."

I already knew we were both committed to this relationship because it was special to both of us. I'd never loved a woman before, and I was a man she couldn't live without. We wanted to get married— someday. We were both willing to sacrifice every- thing to make that happen. But hearing her say it still made my body feel a jolt of happiness.

"So he said he wanted to know me better." She spoke with confidence, but she was obviously tense about my reaction. "So we had lunch for about an hour. He asked me about my father, my relationship with you, and he told me a few things about himself too..."

Even when I was still speaking to my father, we didn't have deep conversations. It was all work and money. "What did he say about himself?"

"He talked about your mom."

He never talked about my mom. "What did he say?"

"That he misses her every day." Titan watched my reaction, paying attention to every single detail on my face. When I gave her nothing but a stoic expression, she moved on. "He wants to make things right with you. He's just not sure how to do that."

"It's been ten years," I said coldly. "He can't make it right."

"Diesel." Her deep tone would set anyone on edge. Her disappointment was packed into the single word. "It could be thirty years, and there would still be a chance. Your father has been making steps toward reconciliation, which is more than I can say for you."

I narrowed my eyes as I watched my woman take my father's side. "I notice how quickly you've forgotten everything he's done. You sweep it under the rug like it's nothing."

"I've never swept it under the rug. Your father didn't handle his grief well, and I've never made excuses for it. But he's always loved you and wanted to do something about it—he just never knew how. Meet him halfway."

"Ten years," I repeated.

"So you're saying he can never be forgiven?" she asked incredulously. "That he doesn't deserve to have his son back in his life? That's what you're telling me?" She leaned farther over the table, developing that fire she possessed in the boardroom. She was disappointed in me, but she was also pissed. "That you won't even try out of respect for your mother?"

The second my mother was mentioned, my hostility dwindled. I respected her in death as much as I did in life. "I just...it's more complicated than that. You see the situation in black and white, but it's deep and painful for both of us. It's not as simple as shaking hands, calling a truce, and going to lunch. He did horrible things to both me and Brett. He's ignored me for ten years. And for the past few months, he's launched a ruthless attack against me. He's stalked my girlfriend and me to dig up dirt on the both of us. He stole my company just to be spiteful. He's threatened me countless times, in my own office. You expect me just to forget about that? Well, I can't. Even if I wanted to, I can't. I can't forget the resentment and the hurt with the snap of a finger. It's not so easy..."

Titan watched me with the same aggressive eyes. "What if he died tomorrow?"

"What?"

"What if he got hit by a bus tomorrow? And you knew he wanted to make things right with you, but you denied him? How would you feel? Would that guilt haunt you for the rest of your life? Yes, it would."

"Titan, he never told me he wanted to make things right. He only talks to you."

Her tense posture softened. "Does that mean you want him to?"

"I didn't say that..." When we'd spoken in my office, he'd told me how angry he was that I'd walked away from him. It was the first time he showed me some kind of affection in years. Before Mom died, we used to throw a football around in the park and get ice cream together. But when she was gone, he didn't have a heart left to love any of us anymore.

"Meet with him, Diesel. Talk to him."

I considered it, but then I quickly changed my mind. "Titan...I don't know."

"What's the harm?"

She didn't understand. "I've already been hurt by him a lot in the past. I don't think I can get my hopes up and be disappointed again. It would kill me. It's easier for me to hate him than hope for the possibility of more."

"Because you still love him," she whispered. "You have to try. You'll hate yourself if you don't."

I hadn't finished my dinner, but I was no longer hungry. I pushed the dish away then ran my fingers through my hair, feeling her intense gaze fixate on my features. "I can't forgive him for what he did to Brett. That's something I can't brush off."

"What if Brett forgave him?"

"That would never happen."

"And what if it did?"

I shrugged. "I don't know. The whole thing is complicated."

"You chose Brett over your father, which I admire. Brett didn't have anyone, and you stood by his side. But don't forget that you lost another brother in the process. Jax is innocent just like you are. You owe it your mother to find your way back to each other."

I'd only spoken to Jax once in the last ten years. I didn't know much about his life anymore. It was a shame that we drifted apart so severely. He chose my father over Brett, but that didn't necessarily make him a bad guy. When we were growing up, Jax was never mean to Brett. "Why are you doing this, Titan? I know you lost your father and you don't want me to experience the same thing...but this is completely different."

"I want you to be happy, Diesel. That's all."

"I'm happy with you. I don't need anything else."

She reached across the table and rested her hand on mine. "I know. But I don't have any family in the world. Thorn was the best thing that I had, and now that he's gone...it's just me. I don't want you to feel alone the way I do, Diesel. You have a father and a brother out there. You should have them in your life."

THORN'S ASSISTANT LOOKED AT ME WITH disappointment. "I already told you he doesn't want to see you in his office again."

"Tell him it's either here or at his front door. His call." I took a seat on the couch and waited. I watched his assistant speak to him on the phone, talking in whispers so I couldn't overhear. She hung up then nodded toward the door, telling me I could walk inside.

I helped myself into his office, seeing him sitting behind his desk typing on his computer. "How's it going?"

He kept his eyes on the screen. "Pretty good until you showed up."

I sank into the chair and watched him.

His fingers tapped against the keyboard as he typed quickly. He was in the middle of an email, so I waited for him to finish. He skimmed through his email quickly before he sent it off. He turned in his chair and faced me. "We're going to have the same conversation we've had dozens of times, so can we do the quick version? I have a lot to do today."

"Forgive her, Thorn."

He sat back in his chair, his arms on the armrests and his gaze focused on me.

"She tries to hide it from me, but she's still miserable."

"Imagine how I feel. I'm still dodging my mother's calls. The world thinks I'm an asshole who was stupid enough to dump Tatum Titan. I can't go anywhere without the press shoving microphones into my face. I went from a respectable businessman to an idiot having a mental breakdown."

"And she feels terrible about all of that."

"Feeling terrible doesn't change my situation," he said coldly. "She made her decision, and I respect it. You need to respect mine."

"You two belong together."

He chuckled and shook his head at the same time. "She'd be marrying me if that were the case. But she wants to marry you—and she's willing to sacrifice everything to make that happen."

I'd always believed they were just friends, but sometimes I wasn't so sure. "Are you in love with her?"

He chuckled again, this time, a little louder. "Really, Hunt? She's yours, and you're jealous of me?"

"I'm not jealous." I had nothing to be jealous of. "I just wonder if that's the real reason you're so angry. I wouldn't blame you, Thorn. She's a remarkable woman. If she left me, I wouldn't be happy about it either."

"I admit Titan is a beautiful woman that I find attractive." He held my gaze, unafraid to speak his mind. "I wanted to be her husband. I wanted to fuck her. I'm not going to sit here and pretend otherwise."

All the muscles in my body immediately tightened in reaction.

"But I've never been in love with her. I've never had romantic feelings for her. It has nothing to do with her—just me. I'm incapable of romantic emotion, which was why losing her was even more unbearable. She was my only chance to have a somewhat normal life. I still want to have a family someday, but now I'm not sure how to do that. I suppose I could find someone else to have an arrangement with me, but I don't trust anyone the way I trusted her." He rubbed his jaw as he worked through his thoughts. "So you don't have anything to worry about, Hunt. My intentions of marrying her were solely based on convenience. But I admit, I did love her as much as I possibly could...more than I've ever loved anyone else. But that love only extends so far... into the realm of friendship."

I believed him. He had no reason to lie to me now.

"I loved having Titan as a partner, someone I could trust implicitly. Finding that kind of relationship in the world in which we live is just not possible. I had something rare, something wonderful. Titan had the moral high ground most businessmen lacked. She had to work twice as hard and be twice as smart to survive in this world, but she did it with grace. She's a role model to me in a lot of ways. I won't lie, losing her has been hard for me. I feel lonely because she was the one person I could be myself around. She knew everything about me, all the good and the bad...but mostly the bad. And now she's gone."

"She doesn't have to be gone, Thorn. She misses you."

He shook his head. "It's over. She betrayed me... and I'll never get over it."

"I hope that's not true."

"It is," he said simply. "I don't hate her. I understand her decision. I want her to be happy...but I can't go back to what we were."

"Maybe you just need some time."

He held my gaze, his blue eyes softening as the sadness took over. "Unlikely."

———

I SHOWERED WHEN I GOT TO HER PENTHOUSE. SHE wasn't home yet, having to work late for Illuminance. I'd already placed a pot roast in the slow cooker so she wouldn't have to worry about making dinner when she got back.

I liked our routine.

She made dinner most of the time, but if she was

busy, I took care of it. We shared our space in harmony, splitting dressers and dividing closet space. I used to have an enormous penthouse all to myself, but I hadn't missed it yet.

When I was out of the shower, I dried my hair with a towel then walked into the bedroom. I reflected on my conversation with Thorn, feeling the annoyance swell inside me. I couldn't believe how difficult it was to put them back together.

Thorn wasn't himself.

He'd turned into a different person. The anger and resentment had turned him into a coldhearted man. I already knew he didn't have affection for most people, and he certainly wasn't compassionate. But I knew he felt differently about Titan.

He was devastated.

But I wouldn't give up. Titan needed him in her life, and I knew he needed her too.

I'd figure it out—eventually.

Just when I pulled on my sweatpants, she stepped into the bedroom. She was still in her sky-high heels, wearing her black dress with a white gold necklace. Her satchel was left by the door, and she turned to me with a smile on her face. "Something smells good."

When I looked at her, I didn't think about dinner,

Thorn, or anything else. All I thought about was her beautiful lips, painted red with her lipstick. I thought about the way her gentle breaths would fill my mouth. That small tongue always drove me wild, whether it was in my mouth, against my cock, or dragged across my chest.

I moved into her and immediately dug my hand into her hair. My mouth sealed over hers, and I kissed her, getting lost in the lustful embrace. My tongue immediately went into her mouth, escalating the passion before she even had a chance to breathe. I hooked my arm around her slender waist, and I dragged her into me, feeling the shape of her breasts through the soft fabric of her dress.

Her arms wound around my neck, and she pulled herself higher on her toes so she could kiss me harder. She matched my intensity instantly, her nails pressing into me with aggression. She knew what she wanted, and she wasn't afraid to take it— just the way I did.

I guided her to the bed and lowered her back to the mattress. I stood at the foot of the bed and shoved my sweatpants and boxers down until my thick cock popped out. I yanked her panties off, and I shoved her dress around her hips.

I gripped her ass and dragged her to the edge of

the bed, positioning her so she could take my cock deep and hard. I shoved myself inside her with a deep thrust, pushing all the way inside until every inch of my cock was sheathed.

She responded with a moan. Her nails dug into my forearms, and she gasped as if she'd never felt me like this before.

My hands gripped the back of her thighs, and I pinned her perfectly underneath me, her legs spread and her pussy ready for me. I thrust into her hard, fucking her like I hadn't just had her that morning before work.

Her fingers locked around my wrists, and she dragged herself back to me, taking in my cock as I gave it to her. "Diesel..."

I stepped closer to her, hitting her deep.

She moaned harder, her head rolling back as she released a quiet scream.

I pumped her with come every morning, every afternoon, and every night. I wanted her to be stuffed at all times, to overflow with my desire.

She moved her hands up my chest, her hair stretched out across the mattress around her. Her green eyes were wild with fire, and her beautiful lips were parted in ecstasy. "I love you..."

That was the biggest turn-on of all. I leaned over

her and shoved my hand into her hair, getting a tight grip on her so she couldn't slip away. I rolled my hips harder so I could pound into her with the same aggression. "I love you too, baby."

She sat beside me on the couch, her legs resting over my thighs. She was in my t-shirt and a fresh pair of panties, her hair still messy from the way I'd wrapped it around my fingertips. Dinner was in our bellies, so we enjoyed a glass of wine in front of the TV.

Titan was all over me—all the time.

I loved it.

Her hand rested across my chest, and she placed her chin on my shoulder. It wasn't comfortable for her to watch TV that way, but she'd rather be on me than anywhere else. "Diesel?"

My hand moved up and down her thigh. "Yeah, baby?"

Her hand glided down my chest toward my torso. Her fingers felt cold against my skin, probably because I always ran a few degrees warmer than her. I could be shirtless and barefoot but still perfectly comfortable. She could be deep under the covers in bed and still shiver. "Did you read my father's book?"

The question caught me off guard. It was the last thing I expected her to ask. It took me a second to comprehend the situation, to try to understand what would make her ask me that. I had the book in my nightstand. Maybe she opened the drawer one day and discovered it. But she hadn't been at my place in a while, so this must have happened some time ago. "Most of it."

Her eyes softened in the special way they only did for me. A slight smile formed on her lips. "Why?"

"I wanted to get to know him—and you."

"What did you think?"

"I enjoyed it. He was a great poet."

"Really?" she whispered, her eyes burning with emotion.

"Yeah." I squeezed her thigh. "I felt like I was reading an autobiography of his life."

"I organized the poems that way...putting them in order."

I remembered one poem in particular. It was the last one I read. It was too emotional for me to continue. "My favorite was 'Remember Me.'"

The touched expression on her face died away as the tears welled in her eyes.

I knew exactly what it was about as I read it. He was diagnosed with cancer and knew he didn't have much time to accept it. He expressed all his fears. He was afraid to die and face what was next, but he was more afraid of what would happen to his daughter when he was gone. He didn't know who would take care of her. And he didn't want her to remember the final months of his life, but instead, remember the good times they had. "I could feel how much he loved you."

Tears broke free, but sobs didn't accompany them. She wiped her tears with the back of her forearm, quickly bringing herself back to a sense of calm. "He did."

"He'd be proud of you, you know," I whispered.

She nodded. "I do."

I placed my palm against the back of her head and pulled her into me, placing a kiss on her forehead. "How did you know I was reading it?"

"I found it in your nightstand." She wrapped her arm around my neck as she held on to me. "I wasn't snooping...just looking for painkillers."

"I don't care if you look through my things. I have nothing to hide."

"Even if you don't care, I respect you and trust you too much to do that."

My body flushed with an underlying sensation of heat. Just as I fantasized about her naked on my bed, I imagined this kind of foundation between us. I loved the way her voice didn't flinch when she said those words. Like there was no longer a doubt in her mind, she trusted me implicitly. "That means a lot to me."

"And it means a lot to me that you read his poems."

"I wish I'd had the chance to meet him. Seemed like an amazing guy."

"He was," she said with fondness. "All he wanted was to give me a better life."

"And I think he succeeded." I kissed her on the forehead again, nuzzling her with affection. I'd never caressed a woman with my lips like this. I used to see women as sex objects. All I wanted to do was fuck them and forget about them. While I viewed Titan as the sexiest woman in the world, I saw so much more. I saw the woman I wanted to wake up to every morning.

"He did. And you make my life even better."

3

TITAN

Two weeks had come and gone.

No word from Thorn.

It was the longest we'd ever gone not speaking to each other.

The love of my life was back, and my world felt more complete—but there was something missing. Thorn was the only family I had in the world, and it didn't feel right not sharing my life with him.

I missed him.

I wondered how often he thought about me.

I wondered if he missed me too.

My mind drifted away to the last conversation I had with him in his office. He'd turned to his computer and silently dismissed me, like I meant nothing to him. Just weeks before that, he stopped looking at other women in my presence because he wanted to be committed to our relationship. I thought about those things as I entered the coffee shop and searched the sea of tables.

Brett waved at me from the corner. He wore a smile that reminded me of Diesel's. Their features weren't as similar as those Diesel shared with his father, but there was still an obvious likeness.

I reached his table and sat down. He already had a coffee waiting for me.

"You seem like someone who takes your coffee black."

"I do, actually."

He tapped his fingers against his temple. "I read people pretty well. So what's up? Are you interested in my new lines of cars?"

"Yes. But that's not why I asked you to coffee."

"Then, why?" he asked. "You want some advice about my brother?"

I was certain Diesel had already told him we were back together, so I didn't bother explaining it. "No. I have no trouble handling him."

He grinned. "You're all woman. That's why."

"I actually wanted to talk to you about something else...and you aren't going to like it."

"I doubt it," he said. "The only two things I hate to discuss are war and Vincent Hunt. As long as you steer clear of those two subjects, my mind is wide open." He sipped his coffee, wearing a leather jacket with an olive t-shirt underneath.

I gave him an awkward smile back. "Well..."

His eyes narrowed as he cocked his head to the side. "What is it, Titan?"

"It's Vincent Hunt that I want to discuss."

Every sign of happiness instantly dropped from his face, replaced by a stone-cold expression. The steam from his coffee wafted toward the ceiling, hot and ready to be enjoyed. He kept his fingers around the sleeve but didn't take a drink. "He's still pulling his usual bullshit?"

"No. Actually, he's called a truce."

Brett scoffed before he took a sip. "A temporary one."

Now I knew how this conversation was going to go. "I've been spending some time with him lately."

"In court?" he jabbed.

"No. We had lunch together last week."

He cocked an eyebrow when he realized how this conversation was going. "You're serious?"

"Yeah. He told me he wants to make amends with both you and Diesel."

"Amends?" He said the word like he didn't know what it meant. "Why?"

"Because you are family."

"I'm not," he said. "Never have been and never will be. But I'm okay with that. If he and Diesel can work things out, good for them. Based on the things Diesel's told me, it doesn't seem likely. But you never know."

"Jax is your brother too."

"We've drifted apart."

"You're still brothers."

He shrugged.

"And Vincent would like to have a relationship with you...if you're willing."

He released a laugh like I'd made some ridiculous joke. "Cut the shit, Titan."

I didn't know if I'd ever be able to help Vincent. He might have done too much damage. Brett could hardly take me seriously. "No bullshit, Brett. He said those words to me."

"Why? He never liked me."

"That's not true."

"No offense, Titan, but you weren't there. Trust me, I know how he felt about me."

"And he feels bad about that now. He wants to start over."

"I'm not his son, so I don't see why."

"But you're his wife's son...and he wants to be involved in your life."

He shook his head. "I have my own life. I don't need some old man pretending to care about me. I'm not a child anymore."

"He's not trying to be a father to you. He just wants to be part of your life."

Brett drank from his cup, silently dismissing the conversation.

"Would you be willing to meet with him? Get a drink?"

"No." He gave his answer before I even finished speaking. He wiped it off the table, shut down the possibility altogether.

"Brett—"

"I don't owe him anything. He doesn't owe me anything."

"He wants to make things right with Diesel. In order to do that, he has to work on your relationship first."

"So he's just using me?" he demanded.

"No. But it's the first step. You should at least sit down with him and talk to him."

"Why?" he demanded. "The second I turned eighteen, he kicked me out. I went to public school, while my brothers were given everything they wanted. We didn't even celebrate my birthday."

How could Vincent stoop so low? "He has an explanation for that. I think you should listen to him."

"Why are you doing this, Titan?" he countered. "After what he's done to you, this doesn't make sense."

"This isn't about me. This is about you and Diesel. I know what it's like not to have a family, and if there's any chance that all of you could reunite, we have to try. Vincent is sorry and would like the opportunity to tell you that to your face. Give him the chance."

Brett looked down at the table and rubbed the back of his head. He'd always been friendly and sweet with me, treating me like a lady but respecting me like a male at the same time. He had a big heart. I could see it in his smile. Despite what he went through, he still shone with a beacon of hope. "No."

"Brett, come on—"

"I said no." He drank from his cup again, taking a large gulp despite how hot it was. "And I don't want to talk about this anymore. I don't ask about your private life or your issues with family...so let's drop it."

"Did Diesel tell you about my family?"

He lifted his gaze and looked at me. "No."

"My mother left after I was born. Overcome with the responsibility of the title, she couldn't handle it and took off."

His eyes softened in sympathy.

"My dad died of cancer before I turned eighteen. Not a single relative shares this planet with me. I'm entirely alone, and it's very difficult sometimes."

He stared at the table, unable to meet my gaze.

"I don't want that for you and Diesel."

"We have each other," he mumbled.

"But you could have more."

He fingered the sleeve around his coffee cup, his eyes directed on what he was doing. "Can I ask you something?"'

Since we were talking about something so personal to him, I should reciprocate. "Of course."

"If your mom showed up on your doorstep and apologized, would you forgive her?"

No one had ever asked me that before, and I'd never even considered the possibility. I could have tracked her down because I had her name, but I'd never wanted to. She chose to leave, to remain anonymous. Tracking her down wouldn't change the past, and it wouldn't change the present either.

Brett lifted his gaze and looked at me, his eyes scanning back and forth as he stared into my eyes. He waited for an answer, wondering what I would say.

I wanted to lie and say what he wanted to hear to accomplish my objective, but I couldn't lie about something like that. "I don't know what I would do, Brett. I've never considered the possibility before. But the situations aren't the same. Vincent could have placed you in foster care, but he never did. He still took care of you...he didn't abandon you the way my mother abandoned me."

THE MEDIA WAS SCRUTINIZING THORN EVEN MORE, making me look like the heartbroken angel. My plan wasn't to come out on top, to use this publicity stunt to my advantage, but unfortunately, it seemed it was going that way.

Thorn was looking worse with every passing day.

Manwhore.

Heartbreaker.

Cheater.

Liar.

A bunch of things that didn't exemplify his character at all...except the manwhore one.

I couldn't take it anymore.

I was sitting at my desk when I called him.

Ring.

Please answer.

Ring.

Come on.

Ring.

He's not going to answer...

Voice mail.

I hung up without leaving a message and ran my fingers through my hair. The stress of the situation was weighing me down, making me feel like I was sinking directly into the earth. The dirt was rising, and soon I would be buried six feet under.

I wished I could fix this.

Jessica spoke through the intercom. "I have Mr. Vincent Hunt on line one."

"Thank you, Jessica." I spoke with my eyes closed, swallowing the pain down my dry throat. I didn't want to know what Vincent wanted, probably just an update on what was going on with his son and Brett. I need to shake off this horrible feeling, so I took the call. "Hello, Vincent."

Vincent didn't know me very well, but he was

incredibly observant. He must have read my tone, listened to my painful silence. "Are you alright?"

"Yeah, I'm fine." I immediately changed my tone, forcing myself to sound casual and authoritative at the same time. "What can I do for you?"

He let his silence stretch on for nearly thirty seconds.

If it were anyone else, I'd wonder if we became disconnected. But with Vincent, silence was his main form of conversation.

"You can talk to me, Titan."

Something about his deep voice was reassuring to me. Maybe it was because it reminded me of Diesel. Or maybe there was something fatherly about his tone. It reminded me of my own father, something he would have said to me if he were still alive. "I'm just going through a hard time right now..."

"I hope this doesn't have anything to do with Diesel."

"No."

"I'm listening."

"I'm sure you're busy, Vincent."

"I'm never too busy for you, Titan."

I thought of my father again, feeling like I was stepping back in time. "When I broke things off with

Thorn, he was really upset about it. Publicly, there wasn't a good way to end things. I thought you were going to leak those photos of me, so we decided to have Thorn leave me. Now the world hates him..."

"I've noticed."

"And it breaks my heart because it's my fault. I told him I wanted to be with Diesel. He said he couldn't forgive me for that." I looked out the window, seeing the sunshine and the cloudless sky. "He's the closest thing I've ever had to family. It's been hard losing him...I feel like I lost a piece of myself."

"I'm sorry to hear that," he said quietly.

"I've called him a few times, but he doesn't answer. I've already apologized as many times as I can...but it doesn't matter to him. Honestly, I can't blame him for being so angry. But if I went back in time, I would have made the same decision anyway..."

"I can talk to him."

I'd never expected him to make an offer like that, to get involved in my life when he had more important things to do. "I appreciate that, but I don't think it would matter. Diesel has already tried, but nothing worked."

"I see..."

I sat on the phone with him, letting the silence linger. It was something I did with Diesel and no one else. It surprised me how comfortable I became with Vincent when he'd been my enemy just a few months ago. He'd hurt the man I loved, but now I saw him as a confidant.

"You want my advice?"

"Sure."

"Thorn is in a difficult situation. His reputation has been ruined. He's lost the one person he can count on. The world is against him..." He paused into the phone. "When your story was hot in the press, Diesel dragged our family problems into the mix. He did it to spare you, even though he humiliated me in the process. He made a sacrifice that launched a war with a dictator. His actions were admirable but also risky. I suggest you do the same for Thorn."

I stared at my desk as I considered what he'd said. It wasn't bad advice. Honestly, I wondered why I hadn't thought of it before. "So I should go to a press with a story that will distract the media?"

"Yes. But if you want to prove how much your friendship means to you, you need to incriminate yourself. Protect his reputation and ruin your own. It may not work. Maybe too much damage has been done. But it might be enough."

"What story should I reveal?"

"How about you and Diesel? You can tell the world that you fell in love with someone else. Thorn was hurt and left. He did what anyone else would do and turned to booze and women. If you spin it right, you can make this romantic, that you loved Thorn but found your soul mate. It'll probably make you look bad, but at least it'll make Thorn look good."

"That's not a terrible idea..."

"You're a very powerful woman, Titan. Your image means a lot to women everywhere. It's because of you that women are standing up to domestic abuse more than ever before. It's because of you that women feel empowered enough to do anything. It's because of you that more women are entering the workforce than staying at home. You're a symbol for independence and feminism. You would be tarnishing that reputation. You would be destroying something you worked so hard for. You would make the world believe in a lie that doesn't reflect who you really are. It's a terrible sacrifice, a very painful one. So you're the only one who can decide if your friendship with Thorn is worth it."

I knew the answer within a heartbeat. "Yes. He's worth it."

"Then you have your answer, Titan."

BRETT WASN'T AS THRILLED TO SEE ME AS HE USUALLY was. He wore a faint scowl, and his invisible walls were erected high. He had agreed to lunch with me, but he did it hesitantly. He sank into the chair across from me, wearing that guarded expression that reminded me of Diesel's.

"Thanks for meeting me."

"I hope you want to discuss cars this time."

"I do like cars." I felt bad for what I was about to do, but it seemed necessary. If I didn't push myself into the situation, nothing would get resolved. All three of these men would repeat their behavior indefinitely.

"Good. Because that's all I want to talk about."

"What about women?" I teased.

He lightened up a bit. "I'm not talking about that in front of a lady."

"Come on, I'm not a lady," I said with a laugh.

"Yes, you are, Titan. It's a distasteful topic."

"You think Thorn never mentions those things?"

I questioned. "Trust me, I've heard stories you can't even imagine..."

A smile broke through. "That's a good point."

"So, what's going on in the love department?"

"Love?" he asked with a raised eyebrow. "Absolutely nothing. There's never anything going on in that department. Now, the *women* department is a totally different story..."

"Then there's a lot of action?"

"A bit," he said. "But I've never been the kind of guy to run my mouth about it."

"That's the gentlemanly thing to do."

"And if you're wondering, Diesel never runs his mouth about it either."

I wasn't wondering at all. I knew Diesel would never share our most intimate moments with someone else. "I know."

"But he does talk about you...a lot."

"I hope he says good things."

"Only good." He finally picked up the menu, dropping his guard.

Vincent rose from a nearby table and walked toward us. In a black suit and wearing a dark look, he disturbed the air around him. He had a heavy presence that everyone took notice of. It wasn't just his height and strength that captured everyone's attention. It was the natural authority he possessed. He pulled out the chair beside me and took a seat.

When Brett heard the chair move, he looked up from his menu.

And froze in place. He stared at Vincent as if he couldn't believe what he was looking at. He continued to hold his menu, but he gripped it a little tighter like a lifeline. Brett's approachable countenance was long gone, replaced by a guarded expression that was ten feet of solid concrete.

Vincent sat with a straight back and a rigid posture. He was naturally intimidating, which didn't help in a situation like this. He stared at his stepson, his expression unreadable. In a crisp suit with a hundred-thousand-dollar watch on his wrist, he reeked of power and money.

The men continued to stare at each other.

I waited for someone to speak, to say what was on their minds.

But like two hostile animals locked in a cage together, they observed each other like prey.

This wasn't how I wanted things to go, so I spoke. "I'm sorry I lied to you, Brett."

"You didn't lie to me," he said coldly. "You tricked me."

"Whichever you want to put it...I'm sorry. You've

made your feelings for Vincent perfectly clear, and I know you aren't interested in a reconciliation. But I think the two of you should at least have a conversation. You say Vincent doesn't mean anything to you, but I know you must be harboring some pain from your childhood."

"No," Brett said coldly. "I got over it pretty quickly." He finally grabbed his water and took a drink.

"Diesel says you're very fond of me."

Brett's hostility dipped slightly.

"Which means you trust me. Or am I mistaken?"

All he gave was a slight nod.

"Well, this is important to me. Please just talk to Vincent for fifteen minutes. You never have to see him again if you don't want to."

"Until you trick me again."

I gave a slight smile. "No more tricks."

Brett rested his back against the chair then turned his head in Vincent's direction. "I'm listening."

Here we go.

If Vincent was nervous, he didn't show it. His posture remained stiff like it usually was, and his breathing didn't escalate at all. It still surprised me how similar he was to Diesel. Not only did they look alike, but their behaviors were nearly identical too.

"Indifference is far more cruel than hatred. Indifference implies you don't think about me at all. Hatred indicates you think about me often...which gives me hope. You still care, and as hard as it is to believe, I still care too."

I listened to his deep voice, taken off guard by the philosophical beginning. Vincent Hunt continued to surprise me.

"I'm not going to make excuses for what I did, Brett. I can give you my reasons, my justifications. I can tell you that I was devastated when I lost your mother, so broken I completely lost my grip on reality. But that doesn't change anything. I can tell you it had nothing to do with you, but that still wouldn't make a difference. I didn't treat you with the love and respect that you deserved, and I apologize for that. Even if you do forgive me, it won't be enough to fix the pain in my chest. I know your mother is disappointed in me, and if I'm ever lucky enough to see her again, she won't be thrilled to see me."

I watched Brett stare at Vincent, focusing on his words without blinking.

"I want you to know it wasn't you," Vincent continued. "I'm the only one to blame for the situation. I struggled to accept the fact that there was another man in your mother's life. Every time I looked at you, I saw her face—but I never saw mine. I'm a very jealous man when it comes to your mother. I'd never known the emotion before, never cared enough to be possessive of anyone. But knowing your mother ever loved a man besides me... never settled with me well. So every time I looked at you...I was reminded of a past I was never part of. I lost your mother at such a young age that I wished I'd had her longer, had known her sooner. This explanation isn't an excuse or a justification. I just want you to know it had nothing to do with you."

Brett was silent, and it didn't seem like he was going to say anything.

"I know you're a grown man now. You're very successful, and you built a business from the ground up. You stood on your own two feet, and I'm very proud of you for that. I'm proud of Jax and Diesel as well, but they used my wealth to get where they are now. You had nothing but the dirt below your feet. You should be proud of that. I know I am."

Brett gave a slight reaction, but it seemed like he was trying to fight it.

"If I were you, I wouldn't care about having a relationship with me either. It's been a long time, and you don't owe me anything. There was never a bond between us. If you want to go back to pretending I don't exist, I can't say I blame you. But I would like to get to know you, Brett. I would like to have a relationship with you. We can't erase the past, we can't forget the pain I caused you, but we could have something entirely new."

Brett finally spoke. "Why?"

"Why what?" Vincent asked.

"Why do you want a relationship with me at all?" He didn't ask the question in a hostile way.

Vincent stared at him with his dark eyes, his shoulders broad and strong. He hadn't moved since the moment he sat down, and he looked as immobile as a statue. "Because you're my son. We may not be related, but we're family. Your mother loved you with all her heart, and I still love her so much it hurts. I want to make up for the time we lost. I want to make your mother happy. I want to be a father to you—if you'll let me."

Brett shifted his gaze away, looking out into the restaurant with a hard expression on his face. Like Diesel, he wiped his emotions away and left nothing behind. Whether he was touched or hurt, he didn't show it.

I was almost on the verge of tears from listening.

"I was never a good father to you, so I understand if that's not what you want. I'm more than happy to be your friend instead. Whatever you want, Brett."

Brett still didn't speak.

I waited for something to happen, for some kind of movement.

Vincent was patient, silent and unmoving.

Brett thought to himself for nearly two minutes, the expression on his face hard. "You did a lot of terrible things..."

"I know," Vincent said.

"I'm not sure if I can get over that."

Vincent hid his disappointment. "I understand."

I shouldn't intervene, but I had to. "Brett, please. You can take it slow. Your relationship doesn't need to change overnight."

"You don't understand, Titan," Brett said quietly.

"I do understand," I said. "I don't have a father, and that hurts every single day. I want you to have everything I wish I had."

Brett still wouldn't look at me. "I don't have an answer right now."

I couldn't let this fall apart. "Brett—"

Vincent placed his hand on my arm, gently silencing me. "Be patient. Brett has been through a lot. He can take all the time he needs. And if he wants nothing to do with me, I'll respect his decision."

I swallowed my disappointment, but it didn't move far down my dry throat. We sat in silence together, Brett still refusing to look at either one of us. After a few minutes trickled by, Brett rose from his seat. "I need to be somewhere." He walked out of the restaurant without looking back.

I sighed in defeat, disappointed even though my expectations weren't high. "I wanted that to go differently."

"I thought it went well, actually."

I turned to him in surprise.

"I didn't even expect him to listen to me. Just like his mother, he's compassionate. Makes me feel more ashamed of what I did to him."

4

HUNT

I DIDN'T MENTION Thorn to Titan since it always made her upset. Even when I didn't bring him up, she was usually thinking about him. After our conversation died away, a fleeting look of sadness would come into her expression.

But now I had something to say. "I have an idea to get you and Thorn talking again."

"You do?" She sat across from me at the dinner table, ignoring her food and enjoying her wine. She didn't speak with much enthusiasm, as if she had little belief that I could contribute anything worthwhile.

"It's not the best idea. I'll say that up front."

"I'm listening."

"The one thing that brings people together is tragedy. So if he thought something bad happened to you..." I knew Thorn would drop everything he was doing if he thought she was in danger. He killed someone to protect her. That kind of loyalty existed far beneath the surface. It was something that couldn't be erased, even after a decade of silence had passed.

She held her glass of wine in her hand but didn't take a drink. "You think I should lie to him?" She couldn't keep the tone of incredulity out of her voice. She detested the idea, the disgust written all over her face. "I'd never do that."

"I didn't say it was a good idea. But it's all we have. I've tried talking to him a few times...he won't budge."

She took a long drink of her wine. "He's pretty upset with me. Never takes my calls."

I hated this. I hated it so much. I didn't blame Thorn for his decision because he was the one who got screwed over, but I still thought they should work this out. Titan was forced to make a terrible decision, and she didn't have much to work with.

"Thorn cares about me too much. I would never do that to him."

I had to respect her decision.

"Anytime I'm down, he immediately asks... Never mind."

I suspected I knew what she was going to say. "Then forget I said anything."

She swirled her wine before she took a drink. "I keep waiting for it to get easier...but it never does."

"We'll figure it out, baby. He can't stay mad forever."

"He's not a stubborn man...that's what bothers me."

I took a bite of my dinner, chewing slowly as I watched the forlorn expression on her face. She was happy with me, showed me that beautiful smile every day. But she could be complete if she had her best friend in her life.

"I have to tell you something." She pushed her plate to the side, dismissing it.

"I'm listening." When she took that tone, it didn't necessarily mean something was wrong. Sometimes she was just getting right to the point, turning professional.

"I arranged for your father and Brett to talk this afternoon."

I'd assumed she would mention Stratosphere or something else business-related, not that. "Brett agreed to meet him?"

"No." She wore a slightly guilty expression. "I kinda ambushed him..."

I appreciated her concern, but she was taking it too far. "Baby, you need to back off. You relayed the message to both Brett and me. Now it's our turn to decide how we'll handle things."

"Both of you refuse to see him."

"And that's our decision."

"Well, it's the wrong one."

My eyes narrowed on her face. "Excuse me?"

"You've interfered in my relationship with Thorn countless times. Would I have approved of it at the time? No. But I'm glad you did it. It's the same thing here."

If she hadn't thrown that in my face, I would be angry by her actions. But for fear of sounding hypocritical, I didn't argue. "How did that go?"

"Your father said some powerful things. I think it got to Brett."

"He's a master manipulator…"

"But he wasn't manipulating. He was being genuine. And I think that's why it affected Brett so much."

"Why do you think it affected him like that?"

Titan held my gaze, her will strong and unbreakable. Her fingers rested on her glass, but her slender shoulders were still perfectly straight. The harder she became, the more beautiful she appeared.

Loving her had taught me what I liked in a woman. She was vastly intelligent, fiercely independent, and insanely strong. She wasn't some helpless woman who needed a man for anything. The only person she needed was herself. "Because he listened."

She schooled me at my own game, saying just a few words to get the impact to sink into my veins. I imagined how their conversation went, my father sitting across from Brett in a public restaurant. I hadn't seen them in the same room since we were younger. It was almost impossible to believe. "Did Brett say anything?"

"He said he needed to think about it."

I tried to hide my surprise but I couldn't. Brett had been treated worse than I had. I would have expected him to punch my father in the face then storm out. The fact that he sat there, listened, and then said he would consider everything...left me in disbelief.

"Which brings me to my next point..." She pushed her glass away too, her slender arms stretching across the table. Her nails were candy-apple red, the color complementing her fair skin. She was another suit in a corporate world, but her feminine touches made her stand out. "I want you to speak to your father."

I tried not to laugh. "Not gonna happen."

"We can do this one of two ways." She held up two fingers. "One..." She lowered one digit. "I can arrange for you to meet him without your knowledge, and you can be bombarded when you least expect it."

I knew it wasn't a bluff.

"Two...we could sit down together and get through it." She pulled her hands back toward her body. "How do you want to do this, Diesel?"

I felt like a competing executive across the boardroom. My balls were in her hands, and she knew it. "I've never wanted to fuck you more."

She hesitated slightly, her eyes shifting in response to my bluntness. "Is that a yes?"

I'd rather be aware of the meeting than walk into it blindly. "You aren't giving me much of a choice." I pushed the chair back as I rose to my feet. My cock was hard in my sweatpants, and I tugged my bottoms off as my enormous cock revealed itself.

She didn't take her eyes off me, but she licked her lips.

"I'm gonna fuck you so hard, baby."

"I'm not seeing the downside to this."

I shoved everything off the table, making plates and glasses shatter against the hardwood floor. I was pissed, so I didn't care about respecting her property, and judging by the darkness in her eyes, she didn't give a damn either. "When you're sore tomorrow, you'll think otherwise."

AFTER I HIT THE GYM, MY DRIVER TOOK ME TO TITAN'S penthouse. I was surprised the paparazzi hadn't photographed me going to her apartment all the time. Since neither one of us left the building after we came home from work, photographers probably didn't catch anything.

I was getting into the back seat when Brett called me.

I knew what this was about. "Titan told me what happened."

Brett didn't change the subject. "She ambushed me, man. I thought we were just getting lunch and...boom."

"It was pretty sleazy."

"Sneaky is a better description. We met a few days before that, and I told her I wasn't interested in reconciling with Vincent. That's probably why she pulled the stunt."

"She doesn't stop until she gets what she wants."

"I feel bad for you..."

Even if this situation annoyed me, I was still a very lucky man. "You don't need to feel bad for me, man." Her determination to bring us all together because she lost her own father was frustrating, but there were worse things. I still loved everything about her, even the things I hated. "What did he say to you?"

"He apologized."

"That's surprising."

"He said a few other things...that he's disappointed in himself. He let Mom down. He's ashamed of his behavior...it goes on."

"And you believe him?"

"I'm not sure. But I can't see what else he gets out of this. It's not like I have something he wants."

"True..."

"We were never close before, so it's hard for me to imagine having any kind of relationship with him."

"Then don't."

"Yeah...I don't know."

The fact that my brother wasn't outright rejecting the idea was surprising. "I'll support whatever you decide."

"I know. Has he spoken to you yet?"

"No, not yet. Titan said it's coming."

"Yeah...I'm sure it is."

The car stopped in front of Titan's building. "I should get going. We can get a beer tomorrow if you want to talk about it in more detail."

"No. I want to think about it some more. I'll call you."

"Alright."

"Bye." He hung up.

I took the elevator to the top floor then walked inside Titan's penthouse. The smell of dinner was in the air, and there was no evidence there had been a mess on the floor just last night. "What smells so good?"

She was sitting on the couch with her heels lying on the rug. Her eyes were glued to her laptop, obviously still working. But when I stepped into her home, she put her computer aside and greeted me at the door.

With a sexy kiss.

She spoke into my mouth as she kissed me. "Me."

I smiled against her mouth before I kissed her again. My hand fisted her hair, and I pulled her harder into me, loving the feeling of her plump tits against me through her top. I sucked her bottom lip then gave her my tongue, my cock hardening in my gym shorts. Now I got great sex every morning, every night, and right before bed—with the only woman I'd ever loved.

My hands moved to her tits, and I squeezed them through her blouse. "Missed you."

"I missed you too."

I pulled away and rubbed my nose against hers. "I want you naked on the bed when I get out of the shower. On all fours. Ass in the air."

Her hands snaked up my chest, and she stared at my mouth like she wanted another kiss. "As tempting as that sounds, we have company for dinner."

My fingers dug into her hip, and I wrapped my hand tighter around her hair so I could grip her more firmly. "Who's this company?"

The serious expression in her eyes told me the answer.

"I thought you would give me some notice."

"I just did."

I tugged on her hair gently, pulling her head back so she looked up at me at a better angle. "An hour?"

"If I'd told you this morning, you'd have thought about it all day."

"And we're doing this here?" It was our space, our world away from the reality outside the windows.

"Would you rather do it in public?"

Cameras would swarm us the entire time. There would be inaccurate headlines all over the place the next morning. It would stir up a conversation both of us wanted to bury. "No. I just—"

"It's happening, so it doesn't matter. He'll be here in an hour." She walked away from me, knowing I would release her once she stepped away. She gave me the power to control her, but she knew she could always overpower me whenever she wished.

"You're making this up to me."

She kept her back to me as she walked into the kitchen. "I know."

I REFUSED TO LET ANYONE INTIMIDATE ME— especially a man I hated. In the face of this stressful situation, I could down a few glasses of scotch to soften my nerves, but that would be an admission of discomfort.

I never showed weakness in front of anyone— especially Titan.

I had a strong woman to share my life with. While I admired her wonderful features, her independence as well as her intelligence, I always had to stay ahead of her. I had to be the stronger of the two of us.

I had to deserve her.

So I skipped the scotch.

Titan set the table, placing the salad and entrees onto the hard wood. She knew my father would be there right on the dot, so she was prepared for it.

I watched TV on the couch, pretending it was any other night.

The elevator beeped when my father hit the button.

It was show time.

I turned off the TV and rose to my feet.

Titan walked to the elevator doors and pressed her finger against the button so the elevator would rise. She turned to me next, looking over my expression to see if I was okay.

I walked up to her, staring her down with the same power I always exerted.

"Thank you for doing this."

I watched her lips move, watched the way her eyes lit up in sincerity.

"I know you're only doing this for me...and I appreciate it."

I was wound tight around her finger, paralyzed by her tantalizing kisses. She could get me to do almost anything, and I would obey just to make her happy. She knew she had power over me—but she also knew she was the only person who did. "This is it." I'd have one dinner with him and listen to whatever he had to say. But once the night was over, that was it. I didn't want to revisit this conversation again. "Do you understand me?" My hand moved to her neck, and I felt her pulse against my fingertips. Possessiveness was something I would always struggle with when it came to Titan. Even when no one else was in the room, I needed it to be clear that she was mine.

Disappointment flooded into her eyes. They weren't as vibrant as they were a moment before. Her breathing stopped momentarily, obviously affected by what I said. But she knew she couldn't push me any further. I accommodated her when I could, but I wouldn't bend over backward for anyone. "Yes."

I released her neck the instant the doors opened.

My father stood there in dark jeans and a black t-shirt. He wore a black jacket over his broad shoulders, looking casual but dressy at the same time. I couldn't remember the last time I saw him dressed in something other than a suit. Not a single memory came to mind. He stepped inside and greeted Titan first. "Titan, it's always lovely to see you." He extended his hand.

She took it. "As it is to see you."

My father remained professional with Titan even when he was in her home. I'd never seen him behave inappropriately toward attractive women, but I still appreciated that he didn't do anything more than shake her hand. If he had, I wouldn't have let the affection slide. I wasn't threatened by him, but I didn't want him to think he had any special kind of relationship with her. Sometimes I saw Thorn kiss Titan on the cheek, but that was different. Thorn had earned the right.

My father hadn't.

He turned to me next, appearing just as calm as I was. He was on my turf, stepping into a situation he couldn't prepare for. But that didn't change his suavity, the way he held himself with perfect stature. He didn't extend his hand to shake mine.

Because I wouldn't take it.

"Thank you for your time, Diesel." His hands rested in his pockets, just the way they would if he were wearing slacks. One of his fiercest qualities was his ability not to blink. He blinked far less than the average person, allowing him to hold tense eye contact for a long period of time. He did it now, staring at me almost ferociously. He looked at me like he hadn't seen me in years rather than weeks.

Now that I was face-to-face with him, I didn't know what to say. I didn't want to pretend everything was okay between us because it certainly wasn't. He may have made an impression on Brett, but I wouldn't be so easy. I gave a slight nod in greeting before I turned around and walked to the table.

It was strange seeing my father in Titan's penthouse. This was the place I had dinner with her every night. I had just fucked her on the dinner table last night. It was a secret oasis for both of us, a place where we could hide from the bullshit of the world and just be together. Now one of my biggest enemies was in my holy space.

"Can I get you something to drink, Vincent?" Titan asked as she approached the table.

"I'll have whatever you're having." He moved to the other side of the table and sat down, directly across from me.

I was immediately tense, like he would take a

swipe at me even though he'd never laid a hand on me in my entire life.

Titan filled our glasses with red wine before she took a seat beside me.

The silence was so loud it actually hurt my ears.

The food was hot in front of us, and there was a basket of fresh bread on the table, but no one reached for their fork. My father sat across from me, his arms by his sides and his eyes on me. He gave me the same look he always gave me, examining me like I was an object rather than a person. Maintaining eye contact had never been an issue for him. It was probably where I learned it from.

Titan held her glass of wine in front of her, swirling it gently as she watched the two of us. "I know there are two sides to every conversation, but I think Vincent should go first. Is that okay, Diesel?"

All I did was nod. "I don't have anything to say anyway." I wasn't being purposely hostile, but that was the truth. My father knew exactly how I felt about him. He'd threatened me one too many times.

My father flinched slightly, a reaction other than strength. "First of all, I want to apologize."

It was an apology long overdue.

"You didn't tolerate the way I treated Brett, and you stood up for that belief. It was difficult to turn against your own father, but it was the right thing to do. You defended someone who couldn't defend himself...and I'm proud of you for that."

I didn't have any expectations for this conversation, but that was something I hadn't anticipated. I hadn't imagined he'd feel that way. It seemed like he would always view that final interaction as a betrayal.

"That's the definition of a man, someone who protects the innocent. And you fit that definition perfectly."

He'd always been eloquent with words, and it irritated me that he punctured me with his sincerity so quickly. I expected to be bored by this conversation, not to hang on his every word so deeply.

"My relationship with Brett wasn't how it should have been. It all came down to my own issues, the fact that I was jealous your mother had loved someone else before me. Every time I looked at Brett, I was reminded that she loved another man. If her first husband hadn't died, would she have loved me? I'm not threatened by anything, but that was something that definitely got under my skin. I could never see straight when it came to your mother. I loved her so much that it made me feel emotions I never felt before. As strange as it is to say, I've always been jealous of Brett. Every time I saw your mother love him, it felt like she still loved her first husband too. And that always troubled me. After she was gone...it was even more difficult to be around him. He was like a ghost haunting me, knowing your mother spent time with another man when she could have spent that time with me."

All this time, I had just assumed my father didn't care for Brett because he wasn't his biological son. I didn't realize it came down to jealousy, that he was haunted by the man who came before him. It didn't change my anger, but at least it made him look like less of an ass.

"It's not a justification for my behavior," Vincent said quietly. "But Brett was never the problem. I was."

I stared at him, still quiet.

Vincent took a drink of his wine before he continued. "We didn't speak for a long time...ten years." His chest rose slightly as he took a deep breath. "It may not seem like it, but I thought about you every day. I watched you grow your wealth, watched you start companies and flip others. I watched a younger version of myself dominate corporate America. I may not have said anything to you, but trust me, I was proud."

I shouldn't care if my father was proud of me, but I was. I'd always wanted his approval, ever since I was a boy.

"But my pride and my anger stopped me from doing the right thing. I turned my back on two of my sons, and your mother must have grown more disappointed in me every passing day. If I ever see her again, I know I'm going to get slapped so hard I'll see stars."

He'd be lucky to only get a slap.

"When you told that story about our relationship to the media...I was livid." His body tensed, and he grew visibly angry. His shoulders hunched with tightness. His jawline was a little harder because he clenched his teeth. "I was livid that you shared my greatest mistake with the world. I was angry that the world didn't understand my side of the story. I was hurt that you betrayed me in such a low manner... I lost my temper in a way I never had before."

I refused to apologize for it. It wasn't the smartest thing in the world, but if my father hadn't cast me out for ten years, that never would have happened. Titan was my family, and I had to protect her.

"I didn't know what to do with that anger...so I made a lot of stupid mistakes."

And tried to ruin my life.

My father sighed as he continued to hold my gaze. "I can apologize, but I don't think that will make a difference with you. My behavior was inexcusable. Taking Megaland from you was the least of it. Sabotaging your personal relationship crossed a line. I know that, and I admit it."

I had expected this conversation to be filled with endless excuses. I had expected him to justify his behavior with his own point of view. I didn't expect to hear such a candid and remorseful explanation of everything he did.

He looked at me in silence, obviously finished. He waited for me to say something back.

Titan turned to me, staring at my profile as she waited for a response.

My mouth couldn't form words.

My father narrowed his eyes on my face, not in a hostile way, but in one full of concern. "Talk to me, son."

My chest immediately tightened when he called me that. I hadn't heard him refer to me that way in over ten years. It was a childhood endearment, something he said every time I did something right. When I put away the dishes, he patted me on the back and said, "Good job, son." It was something so trivial at the time, but hearing him say it now made me realize how much it meant to me. He didn't call me Diesel or Hunt. He called me something personal and meaningful.

Words still didn't leave my mouth. I stared at my father and watched him silently wait for words to form on my tongue. Titan waited too, the air around her restless. She wanted my father and me to forget everything that had happened and be a family again. Her heart was in the right place, but her dreams were unrealistic.

"I don't have anything to say."

My father couldn't hide his look of disappointment. The emotion was quick, ending as abruptly as it started, but it happened.

Titan didn't cover up her sigh, her admission of sorrow.

My father's shoulders fell slightly, no longer straight and powerful like a concrete wall.

Titan grabbed my thigh under the table. "Diesel..."

"I told you I would listen to him," I said quietly. "I did as you asked. My promise has been fulfilled." I pushed her hand off my thigh, but the second I did it, I felt like an ass. I had a woman who was going to such lengths to help me, and it was stupid to push her away. I instantly regretted my behavior.

She stared at me with her fiery eyes. "The man you've been at war with is sitting across from you, and he's apologized. You have an opportunity to say how you feel, Diesel. Don't sit there and do nothing."

I stayed quiet.

"Don't be stubborn."

My father stared at me with his penetrating gaze. He hadn't looked at Titan once since the conversation began. His gaze was focused on me exclusively. He'd stared at me before when he'd cornered me in my office, but he hadn't looked at me the way he did now. "Even if you have nothing nice to say to me, I want to know how you feel."

"You want to know how I feel, huh?" I snapped. "I think you're an asshole. That's what I think."

My father didn't flinch, as if he'd been expecting the insult.

"You've come into my office so many times now and threatened me. Plain and simple. What kind of father threatens his son like that?"

He didn't blink.

"And then you went to Titan and tried to buy her loyalty. You knew she meant something to me, but you wanted to burn that relationship too. You wanted to destroy everything around me until I had nothing left. You wanted me to be sad and alone just like you. A father should always want more for his son, not less."

His eyes shifted back and forth as he looked into my gaze.

"And then you blackmailed me... You tried to take away the woman I love." I shook my head. "You think an apology is going to make up for your cruelty? You think some prepared words can erase the past? You think you'll ever give me an explanation good enough to justify your silence for the last ten years?" My voice rose higher and higher with every sentence, my rage swelling.

The powerful look he always gave me was gone, replaced by a face I hadn't seen in a long time. He didn't look like the guarded CEO who was always seeking the upper hand. Now he just looked like a man. "I understand your anger."

"Well, I don't understand yours. I can admit that going to the media about our story wasn't the best idea, but I didn't have much to work with at the time. Titan is everything to me, and I had to protect her. She thought I was responsible for sabotaging her life, and I had to prove to her it wasn't me. I knew my actions would cause a war, but I didn't have any other choice. And I would do it all again, because in the end, I got her. That means more to me than anything else in the world now."

Titan didn't say anything to that.

My father's reaction didn't change.

In apology, I moved my hand to her thigh.

I knew she'd forgiven me when she didn't push it away.

"I understand," my father replied. "But you still could have gone about it in a different way, just as I could have done things better. But pointing fingers now won't change the decisions that have already become part of history."

No, it wouldn't.

"I'm not suggesting we forget the past, Diesel. I'm proposing a new beginning. We can get to know each other again, take things slow. Maybe a lasting relationship will blossom. Maybe you'll never be able to look past my mistakes. But I'd certainly like to try."

I finally broke eye contact, not wanting to look at him anymore. Anytime I thought about my father, I thought about how much I hated him. Now I had to deal with deeper emotions and the fact that he wasn't as evil as he seemed.

"I've apologized, Diesel. I'll never exhibit that kind of behavior again, even if you never forgive me.

You're a grown man who doesn't need the guidance of anyone except yourself, so you don't need a father anymore. But I'd like to be something...even if it's just your friend. You have a brother you never speak to, and even if you can't work this out with me, I'd like you to reconnect with him. You're brothers."

I'd never had a problem with Jax. We became divided in the war. Wanting to avoid each other because all we could talk about was our father, we never spoke. But that distance turned to years of silence. Now we didn't know each other at all anymore. It was a shame to have lost so much time. "Yeah, I'd like to see him."

My father gave a slight nod. "He'd like that too."

Titan placed her hand over mine as it rested on her thigh. "Diesel..."

I ignored her.

She squeezed my hand. "He's done the most he can possibly do to start over. Meet him halfway."

I automatically wanted to snap at her, but I made sure that didn't happen. "It's been ten years, Titan. My father wanted nothing to do with me for ten years. This attempted reconciliation might never have happened if it weren't for you, so does it truly mean anything?"

"It would have." My father inserted himself into

the conversation with his powerful voice. "Because I initiated it when we were in your office. I told you I was hurt that you'd been taken away from me. You're the most important thing in my life. My rage clouded my actions, but my emotions rang true. Titan has made things easier because she's compassionate and understanding. She's helped me reach this point in a much easier way than if I did it alone. As a man, I've never been good with emotions. That was something your mother always helped me with. But I assure you, we'd somehow be having this conversation...even if it took another year for me to make it happen. However, I'm sorry that it took so long. I should have done this the second you walked out the door."

I remembered that afternoon because I was surprised by what he said. At first, I had thought he was talking about Mom, but that didn't make much sense at the time. But when he revealed he was referring to me, that he was so upset I had turned on him, it still had caught me by surprise.

"I know this is hard, Diesel," my father whispered. "Truly, I do. Sometimes, when too much time has passed, it's impossible to find a connection again. We could both go on with our lives and forget about each other, but I suspect we'd be filled with more anger and pain than we already have right now. Maybe it would be the best thing for both of us if we moved forward...one step at a time."

He was a master manipulator, and he was using his talents now. "If you hadn't attacked me for the past few months, maybe. But you did everything you could to take down your own son. I don't think I can just sweep that under the rug."

"I'm not asking you to."

My eyes bored into his.

"I'm just asking you to leave the door open, Diesel," he said. "You don't need to trust me, to forgive me overnight. You don't need to call me your father. All I want is a chance to make this right. You may hate me, despise me for the things I've done. But as your father, I will always love you—no matter how much you hate me."

I couldn't remember the last time he said those words to me. It must have been when I was younger. I thought those words would go right through me without leaving any mark, but they penetrated my heart and stayed in place, like a bullet that didn't exit the body. I tilted my head toward the table and broke eye contact, unable to hold his gaze a second longer.

Silence passed between us. It was heavy with patience, heavy with hope. Titan kept her hand on mine, her small fingers gliding gently over my skin. She didn't pressure me to forgive him, holding her voice this time.

My father kept staring at me. "Son?"

I closed my eyes for a brief moment as I kept my head tilted toward the table. His words surrounded me, suffocated me. I slowly angled my head back up to look at him.

"Please leave the door open."

A part of me wanted to ask him to leave and never come back. A part of me wanted to warn him to steer clear of me. I never wanted to see him again, never wanted to hear his voice again. But another part of me couldn't shut the door. Another part of me felt a flame of hope in my heart. A soft side of me didn't slam the door in his face. It kept my hand steady. "It's open..."

The stern expression on his face immediately died away, replaced by a look I'd never seen before. It was soft, vulnerable, and contained a slight hint of emotion.

"But that's all I can do."

My father straightened his shoulders as he stared at me. He didn't smile, but his expression seemed to soften. There was joy in his eyes, a reflection of ethereal light in the corners. "That's all I ask."

5

TITAN

DIESEL WAS quiet after his father left. He didn't seem angry, but he wasn't himself either. Even though he already had taken a shower when he got home, he took another. I took that as a hint that he wanted some space.

I stayed in the living room and worked on my laptop, giving him all the time he needed. If he were truly angry with me, he would just return to his penthouse and not call me for a few days.

He walked into the living room over an hour later in his black sweatpants that he wore low on his hips. The bottom two abs of his stomach were just as ripped as the six up above. For a man so busy, he still devoted time to his physical fitness. He was thirty-five but had the physique of someone in his mid-twenties.

He made a drink at my bar then took his time coming into the living room. His bare feet thudded against the hardwood floor as he walked. Like a shark that made its presence known in just its silence, he circled the couch as he approached me.

I shut my laptop.

Diesel sat beside me and parted his knees, his long legs stretching out in front of him. He was a large man, tall and built, and he took up a lot of space. My king-size bed felt much smaller when I shared it with someone, but when a man was his size, his chest turned into my mattress.

He took another drink of his scotch before he set it on the coffee table. He sat back, looking at the black TV screen.

I waited for him to speak first so I'd understand his mood better. Right now, he seemed thoughtful and quiet. If he were angry, I'd be able to feel it ooze from his pores. Whenever he was hostile, it was usually easy to notice.

At least, for me.

When five minutes of silence stretched on, it didn't seem as if he was going to say anything at all.

"You still want me to make it up to you?" I whispered, choosing to talk about sex because it was the easiest topic to discuss. The foundation of our rela-

Boss Romance 93

tionship had always been fucking. It was the one thing we always agreed on. Through time, our romance had deepened into the most loving and intense relationship I'd ever known. Sex moved into the background as love took up our focus.

He didn't hesitate before he answered. "Yes."

"And how would you like me to do that?"

His eyes never shifted to me. "Have dinner with me."

"I have dinner with you every night."

"In public."

My heart stopped.

"In a nice restaurant. The two of us holding hands. Not giving a damn what the world thinks of us. That's what I want, Titan. And you're going to give it to me."

That sounded like a dream come true, stepping into the sunlight and letting the world see us for who we really were. But it wasn't the right time, not until I figured out my situation with Thorn. "Okay...in time."

His jaw clenched slightly in anger, but he wasn't as livid as he usually was when it came to this topic.

It didn't seem like he would ever mention his father. "Do you not want to talk about it?"

Silence.

I took that as a yes. "I'm here if you change your mind."

After a long sigh, he spoke. "I don't know how I feel about it."

"Take some time to think it over, and you'll find an answer."

He rested his arm over the back of the couch, his skin lightly pressing against the nape of my neck. "I never expected my father to say any of those things to me. I feel like I'm talking to a different person."

"Because you are. He's different now, Diesel."

"Just a few weeks ago, he was ruining my life," he said in a dark tone. "I don't think people change that quickly."

"They do when they realize what they've lost." I moved my hand to his muscular thigh and felt the hardness under my fingertips.

"He lost me a long time ago…"

"You lost him too."

He turned his face toward me, his gaze looking into mine. "He's right about one thing. None of this would have been possible without you…whether this ends up being a good or a bad decision."

"It'll be a good decision," I said with confidence. "A man can't say things like that and not mean them. Anytime I've been around him, he's been nothing but a gentleman. I believe he has the ability to be a kind person. He just needed some compassion..."

Diesel continued to watch me with his dark eyes, silently wrapping his presence around me. "Not all people deserve compassion, Titan."

"No. But most do."

His fingers moved to my neck, and his thumb rested on my bottom lip. He gently tugged on the skin, sliding his finger down and smearing my lipstick. "I know exactly what I want from you." His thumb traced my mouth, following the curve from one corner to the other. "I want this lipstick smeared around the base of my dick. And I want my come sitting in your stomach. Now."

As the intensity grew between us, the area between my legs began to ache. His fingertips were warm, and the searing gaze he gave me was hot enough to make me melt. My lips parted with the need to obey him, to give him what he wanted. I got his father here because I wanted to repair their broken relationship. But I also liked owing him something...because I knew exactly what he would want as payment. "Yes, Boss Man."

THE INSTANT I STEPPED INSIDE RIO'S, THE HOSTESS recognized me and greeted me with a handshake. "This way, Ms. Titan. Mr. Livingston is already here." She guided me to the table, where Kyle was browsing his menu.

He looked up when he noticed me. "Titan." He rose to his feet and shook my hand.

I did the same. "How are you, Mr. Livingston?"

"Pleased, as I'm sure you are."

We sat down and got straight to business. Our beta testing had revealed how well his products did on my shelves, and conversely, my products had an amazing start on the opposite side of the world. The marketing we did for each other definitely paid off.

"We're certainly hitting the right market without competing with current customers," he said. "We pulled it off, and I'm looking forward to see where this will go."

His products weren't luxury items like mine were. His were directed toward young adults and those in their early twenties. They were made for enhancement, sharpness. My products were designed for women in their late twenties and older. I specialized in skin rejuvenation creams, serums that eliminated crow's feet, and mature makeup that working women in high positions needed to lead their companies. We didn't directly compete with each other, going for markets in different age groups. "As am I. I think we should discuss launching our first real campaign."

"Me too."

We got down to our ideas, and we ordered lunch in between. I had an iced tea and nibbled on a piece of bread as we spoke. I expected Kyle to ask about my public breakup with Thorn, but thankfully, he didn't. Perhaps he understood it was irrelevant to our business venture, and any question he asked would go unanswered.

But then I saw Thorn walk inside. In a gray suit with a black tie, he entered the room and turned heads naturally. Over six feet in height with a handsome face, he would turn heads even if he weren't all over the news.

The hostess guided him to a table, and he was on a trajectory to walk right past me.

Looking at him only reminded me of how much I'd lost. It made me miss our intimate friendship, the way we could tell each other anything and know we would never betray each other's secrets. I missed the way he looked out for me, concern that I never needed and I never appreciated. I missed the way his eyes lit up slightly when he saw me. He didn't usually smile, but that was because he didn't express himself in that way. I was in tune with all of his slight reactions, and I knew exactly what each one of them meant.

He came closer, walking with one hand in his pocket. He scanned the room ahead, looking for whomever he was meeting that afternoon.

Without thinking it through, I rose to my feet to intercept him. I didn't have any expectation for a friendly greeting. The most he might do was look at me. But he wouldn't stop to say more than a few words to me.

But I wasn't thinking.

His eyes turned to me, and his look immediately sharpened as he recognized my features. He obviously hadn't spotted me until that moment, and he couldn't control his surprise. For just an instant, there wasn't the indifference he usually gave me. There was some kind of emotion, some kind of reaction.

He stopped when he was a foot away from me. His other hand moved into his pocket, and a scowl slowly started to form on his face.

I was in the middle of a lunch meeting, but Kyle didn't seem important anymore. One of the two people who meant the most to me was standing right in front of me. I'd do anything to hug him, to know he was my friend. "Hey..." I couldn't fight my expression and the way it fell. I couldn't keep the sadness out of my tone, not even in Kyle's presence.

Thorn turned to Kyle and shook his hand. "How are you, Kyle?"

"I'm well. And you?"

"Never better." He turned back to me, ice-cold. "Titan."

I wasn't the recipient of a handshake. All I got was the cold shoulder as he walked off and headed to his table.

It took me a moment to recover, a moment before I found my seat again. I was aware of some people watching me, curious how my first public encounter with Thorn would go. I faced Kyle again.

He looked at me with sympathy, clearly thinking about everything he'd read in the headlines.

I cleared my throat. "I can get products on the shelf as early as next month."

6

HUNT

I WAS SITTING in my office when Titan called on my cell phone.

I quickly ended the call I was already having just so I could take it. There wasn't a business opportunity lucrative enough for me to make her my second priority. She wasn't my wife, but she felt like family.

The rest of the world could wait.

"Hey, baby." I turned in my chair so I could look out the window and see the overcast sky. It was a cold afternoon in the city, and the forecast anticipated a bit of snow.

"Hey..."

That simple word told me everything. "What happened?"

"I was having lunch with Kyle when Thorn walked in..."

This wouldn't end well.

"He walked by my table, and I stood up to greet him. He said hello to Kyle but ignored me...then walked off."

He was already hated in the media. Ignoring Titan in a room full of people didn't sound like smart publicity. But he obviously didn't care about that, and neither did she. All she wanted was her friend back. I knew Thorn felt the same way, even if he wouldn't admit it. "I'm sorry." I meant those words deeply. They seemed so hollow, an automatic response to sad news. But I meant them every single time I said them to her. I just wished there were something better I could say.

"It doesn't get easier. It only gets harder. I miss him more every day."

If I weren't so secure in my relationship with her, I might be jealous. But she loved me in a way she'd never loved anyone else. She picked me over him because she couldn't live without me. She walked away from a safe and convenient relationship to give our intensity a real chance. "I know you do."

"I have to do something."

"What?"

She never gave me an answer. "I'm sorry to bother you at work. I know you're busy, Diesel."

"Never too busy for you," I whispered into the phone. "You can call me for anything."

"I know...I just don't want to abuse my power. I'll see you later."

I wanted to keep her on the phone a little longer, but my silence wouldn't help her. Sometimes my kisses and touches did the trick, distracted her so she would stop thinking about her pain. But I couldn't do that now. "Alright. Love you." I always held my breath as I waited for her to say it back. I was never afraid she wouldn't repeat the phrase, but I also anticipated how it would make me feel.

It made me feel special.

"Love you too."

"Sir." Natalie spoke into the intercom. "I know you told me to send Vincent Hunt away if he shows up, but...he's refusing to leave."

It'd been a few days since my last conversation with my father. I thought it over a lot, thinking about it while I watched TV on the couch or washed my hair in the shower. I assumed the ball was in my court, and if I wanted to speak to him, I would decide when and where.

I guess not.

"You can send him in, Natalie."

"Alright, sir."

I quickly finished the email I'd been writing and sent it off just as he walked through the door. Back to his aura of natural intimidation, he disturbed the air around him, bringing in silent strength that blanketed everything in his vicinity. He had no reason to be hostile with me, so this was normal with him.

I knew that was how I was with other people too.

He approached my desk with both hands in his pockets. He looked at me straight on, wearing an expression so similar to mine it was strange.

I rose to my feet so we were level with each other. I didn't extend my hand to shake his. Too soon.

"Hey, Diesel. How are you?"

The phrase was so casual, I almost didn't believe it came from him. Most of his greetings were silent threats. It caught me off guard and took a few extra seconds for me to come up with words. "Good. You?"

He didn't answer. "I came by to see if you wanted to have lunch."

Lunch? With Vincent Hunt? Last time we spoke, I agreed to leave the door open. I agreed to give this relationship a chance before shutting the door on the opportunity altogether. But I didn't expect him to come by and ask me to lunch like everything was normal.

We were anything but normal.

I hesitated in my answer, unsure what to do. I hadn't eaten yet because I'd been too busy working. Taking a break for food sounded nice, but I wasn't sure if I wanted to go out with my father like the past was behind us.

It wasn't behind us.

My father stared at me as he waited for me to come up with an answer. "I'll accept no for an answer. Just thought I'd stop by because I just finished a meeting across the street." He pulled his hands out of his pockets and adjusted his watch. "Maybe next time." If he was hurt, he covered up his reaction well. He gave a slight nod before he turned to the door.

Something gnawed at my stomach, a wave of guilt I shouldn't even feel. He was the one who'd made me suffer just a month ago, but now I felt terrible for turning the man down. Watching him try to have a relationship with me made me feel like shit for denying him. "I can spare thirty minutes."

My father instantly turned around, still wearing the exact same expression as before. "That's great. What are you in the mood for?"

I SAT ACROSS FROM MY FATHER AT A TABLE IN THE corner, our drinks in front of us and our entrees on the way. Like the other night, he was staring directly at me, giving me his full focus as if nothing else in the room mattered.

Kinda reminded me of the way I stared at Titan —but different.

My father ordered a scotch even though it was barely past noon. He had always drunk a lot, at least, after my mother died. He drank wine with dinner, but most of the time, he preferred hard liquor. He reminded me of Titan in that regard. His tolerance had built up until the level of being legally drunk had no effect on him.

I stuck with iced tea. I'd told Titan not to drink so much, so I had to stop too—even if she wasn't around.

Now it was quiet like the other night, awkward as hell.

Maybe I shouldn't have agreed to this. "Jax has broken into the solar energy sector." He made the announcement with no warning at all, beginning a conversation like it was strictly business. "He's working with a few engineers from Stanford. They think they have a way to reduce the cost of solar panels by fifty percent."

My eyebrows rose. "That's an insane margin."

"I agree. But he thinks they can do it."

"Have they proven it?"

"In a few ways," he said. "They're still in the developmental stage. It was a risky purchase, but Jax has always been interested in clean energy. He's even proposed a couple of things I can do for my companies all over the world, making them completely green with renewable energy. It'll cost a lot up front, but it'll save me money down the road. Science has always been his interest."

Jax always naturally excelled at science and math when we were in school. I did well in my courses, but I had to work a little harder to understand the same things that came easily to him. Like me, he was quiet and intense, but he had a brain bursting with constant stimulation. He combined his interests in business and science for his corporate pursuits. "He's a smart guy."

"Extremely." His voice held a tone of pride.

Did he talk about me like that too?

"What are you working on now?"

It seemed like this entire conversation would stick to our common interest—business. I was relieved we wouldn't have another repeat of the other night. I couldn't talk about my feelings anymore. "Titan bought me out of Stratosphere, and we're planning on having me return."

"That's a strong company."

"We made a lot of progress together. We both turned it around, and she has ideas that constantly amaze me. If the world knew how smart she really was, people would be even more intimidated."

A slight smile came over his mouth. "I'm already intimidated." My father didn't hide his fondness for her. He seemed to adore her the same way he did Jax.

"She's an amazing woman..." That didn't even scratch the surface of who she was. She lived in a world where she had to work three times as hard to be respected, but not once did she let it get her down. She'd been through a lot for a woman so young, but she never let her past heartbreaks destroy her. She kept her head held high and kept going.

My father took a drink from his glass before he returned it to the table. "When are you going to ask her to marry you?"

It was a very personal question. So personal, I wasn't sure if he even had the right to ask.

My father must have read my mood because he said, "It'd be a mistake not to."

"I don't know, honestly. It's not the best time right now."

He nodded slightly. "Because of Thorn."

"Yeah..." Did she tell him about Thorn?

"She mentioned it to me. We both agree that the only thing that will make Thorn come around is if she does her own interview to take the spotlight away from him. It's not ideal, but her friendship with Thorn is important enough that she's willing to risk her reputation to get him back."

I couldn't keep a straight face because this was all new to me. "When did she say this?"

"A few weeks ago." He kept his eyes on me as he took another drink.

"She never told me that." I felt wounded that my father knew something about her before I did. Why would she tell him and not me?

"I'm sure she was getting around to it. Doesn't seem like she likes talking about him."

I narrowed my eyes. "I can't believe she even told you."

He shrugged with a slight smile on his face. "I think she likes me."

I didn't know what made me more upset, the fact

that she talked to my father about it and not me, or the fact that she had a close relationship with my father at all.

My father dropped his smile as he watched my mood sour. "It wasn't my intention to make you upset."

"What exactly does she plan to say in this interview?"

He sighed, his tone heavy with regret. "I shouldn't have said anything."

"But you did," I snapped. "So now finish it."

"Alright." He finished his drink and returned it to the table. "I told her she should tell the media that she fell in love with you, and while she loved Thorn, you were the man she couldn't live without. Thorn became upset, like any other man would, and he lost control. It'll distract everyone from Thorn and bring the focus on to her."

"And make her look like a cheater and a liar." My voice rose even when I tried to keep it down. "It'll ruin everything she stands for. She has an untouchable image. This will destroy that."

"I know. I warned her of that."

"And she still wants to do it?" I asked incredulously.

He nodded. "We both think it's the only thing

that will make Thorn forgive her. She'd be proving to him that they're still in this together, even if they're apart."

When it came to Thorn, Titan always turned emotional. Just an hour ago, she'd called me and had spoken with a heartbroken tone. She would never be truly happy unless she had both of us in her life again. "I don't want her to ruin everything she's worked so hard for."

He nodded. "I don't either. But Thorn means the world to her."

Now my anger was no longer directed at my father. All I cared about was Titan and how much pain she was in. To even consider this was a suicide mission. "Fuck." I rubbed the back of my neck as I turned my gaze out the window, wishing this nightmare would just end. My love for Titan was still a secret because of this bullshit. Titan didn't deserve to have all of her hard work ruined because she wanted to spend her life with me. It wasn't fair —at all.

My father didn't flinch at my profanity.

"I can't let her do this."

"She's not the kind of woman that you can *let* do anything."

"I'm not letting her destroy her credibility over

this. Thorn should forgive her because she deserves his forgiveness."

My father gave me a look of pity.

I leaned back in my chair as I considered what to do. Once Titan did that, everything would be an uphill battle for her. I could protect her in a lot of ways, but my influence could only do so much. Besides, she wasn't the kind of woman who needed to hide in my shadow anyway. She needed her independence, her own credibility.

Unless I took her place. "I'll do it instead."

"Do what instead?"

"I'll give the interview."

"And say what, exactly?"

"That I was the one who came between them. That I fell in love with her and wouldn't take no for an answer. I couldn't stay away from her, and I made her fall in love with me too. That way, I look like the romantic asshole, people forget about Thorn altogether, and Titan looks like a woman who was swept off her feet."

"I don't think that would have the same effect."

"Why not?" I asked. "It gets the attention off Thorn."

"But that doesn't mean it'll earn his forgiveness. I admire what you're trying to do, and I find it even more admirable that you're both so loyal to each other in every way possible, but it won't mean as much coming from you. It has to be her."

I bowed my head, the defeat washing over me. "She doesn't deserve it..."

"I know. But their friendship means more to her than what the whole world thinks of her."

"Maybe I can talk to him again."

My father shook his head. "Don't interfere with this one. This is about the two of them."

I was definitely going to confront her about it at the very least. "I can't believe she didn't tell me."

"I'm sure she will. Or maybe she was afraid you'd convince her not to do it."

"And she'd be right. That's exactly what I'm going to do."

"There's one bright side to this," he said gently. "Once the world knows her side of the story, there will be no more hiding. You can finally have what you want, Diesel."

That was the only good thing that would come out of all of this. I could have lunch with her whenever I felt like it. We could jog through the park together. I could ask her to be my wife whenever I chose. When we went to conferences together, I could hold her against my side so the world would know she was mine—and the women would know I was taken. "I suppose..."

The silence stretched on until the waiter arrived with our food. He placed the entrees in front of us before he walked off again.

I picked up my fork, but I didn't have much of an appetite.

My father dug in, cutting into his chicken and taking a bite. He watched me eat, not having to watch his own movements to be precise. "I'll say something to Thorn after she gives her interview...to give her a little extra help."

I wasn't sure what effect he could possibly have, but I was surprised he would even offer. "You would do that?"

"I would do anything for that woman," he said simply. "I've always liked her, even before I knew about the two of you. She reminds me of your mother. It's the way she carries herself...the way she talks. She has a natural strength and elegance that your mother always possessed. Something about her comforts me, I can't really explain it. She seems confident that she's going to be a part of your life for a long time. If that's the case, I want to do everything I possibly can to make her feel comfortable. She doesn't have a father of her own...perhaps I can be one to her."

My fingers suddenly felt numb, and I couldn't keep my grip on my silverware. I felt the utensils slightly slide against my moist skin. My father had been a great parent, even after my mother died. But once he pushed Brett aside, all of that changed. Titan had always felt lost without her father. I knew there was nothing she would love more than having someone make her feel like she had family. That was the reason Thorn was so important to her. "Thank you..." The best way to get under my skin was through Titan. Whether my father did that on purpose or not, it was effective. I wanted to give her everything she wanted, and I was willing to do anything to make that happen.

He stopped eating and gave me an emotional look. "You're welcome, son."

WHEN I RETURNED TO THE OFFICE, I MADE THE CALL.

Ring. Ring. Ring. Voice mail.

Why didn't she pick up my call? Maybe she was in a meeting right now. I was certain she would call me back the second she saw my missed call, so I set my phone down and turned to my computer. The second I went to the homepage, I saw the news.

Richest Woman in the World, Tatum Titan, Finally Opens Up About Her Broken Engagement to Thorn Cutler.

Fuck.

I was too late.

I clicked on the link, and I was taken to a live feed. Titan was giving the interview at that moment with one of the biggest broadcasting companies in the nation. She looked exactly the same as she had earlier that morning, in a tight black dress with a white gold necklace around her throat. Her hair was straight today, a curtain of soft hair around her shoulders. Her makeup had been slightly changed for the cameras, but she still looked like the gorgeous bombshell she was.

I turned up the volume.

Denise Thomas was the interviewer, a veteran in journalism. "The entire nation was shocked when we heard the news that Thorn Cutler cut off the engagement. Shortly after that, he was seen with another woman. And we saw your first interaction in Rio's just the other day, where you rose from your seat to greet him and he brushed you off."

Of course, someone recorded that.

Titan kept the same expression, giving nothing away.

"How did that make you feel?" Denise asked.

"Terrible, obviously," Titan said coolly. "Thorn and I have been very close for a long time. Losing him is like losing a piece of myself." Even though this topic made her emotional, she managed to keep a straight face the entire time. She didn't show weakness to the world, only me.

"Then his actions are even worse. He hurt someone he claimed to love."

Titan still didn't react, but she shifted her eyes as if she was about to say something important. "I don't want the world to think Thorn is a bad guy. He's definitely not. The world only sees one aspect of the story, just a sliver of what really happened."

"Then what happened?" Denise crossed her legs and leaned forward.

"The truth of the matter is, Thorn and I were very happy together. He was my best friend...still is. I was very close to his family. Honestly, losing them has been really difficult. But Thorn isn't the one who left. I am."

Denise's eyes narrowed.

"I never meant for this to happen. I love Thorn and always will. We have a strong bond that I can't explain...but then I met my soul mate. I tried to brush it off for a long time, but I couldn't fight it forever. As if something beyond my control was yanking me in a different direction, I had no control over my own actions. With every passing day, my heart began to beat for another man. When it got to the point that I couldn't stop it, I had to tell Thorn the truth. I told him I'd fallen in love with someone else."

Denise didn't keep a straight face as well as Titan did. "Who?"

I moved closer to my computer screen, hoping she would drop my name. I didn't need her to protect my identity from this scandal. I wanted the truth out in the open. People could hate me all they wanted. I didn't give a damn. All I wanted was to be with the woman I loved, no more secrets.

Titan took a long pause before she spoke. "Diesel Hunt."

My lips automatically curved into a smile. Hearing her say my name to the entire world was the sexiest thing I'd ever heard. Warmth washed over me, the soft touch of a tropical tide. There was no going back now. The world knew she loved me, and I loved her.

Denise couldn't contain her shocked expression. "Diesel Hunt?"

Titan nodded. "It happened once we started working together on Stratosphere. At first, I thought it was just chemistry. We did amazing work together. But then the connection strengthened. I could barely be in a room with him without feeling the pull. I kept fighting it, even having him leave the company so I could get him out of my head. But there was no stopping it. I loved Thorn and wanted to spend my life with him...but then I met my soul mate. I didn't know what to do. When I told Thorn, it was the hardest thing I've ever had to do. No one can blame him for acting out like that. Anyone who judges him for his behavior is coldhearted. He's one of the greatest men I've ever known. I could sit here all day and share a million reasons why I love him from the bottom of my heart. He's a gentleman, he's compassionate, he's honest... I would have been very happy with him." Her eyes started to water. "I don't want the world to hate him for something he didn't do. I don't want people to judge him for being upset. I was the one who did something wrong. I was the one who screwed everything up. I'm the one everyone should hate, not Thorn. I'm risking the greatest relationship I've ever known for something that's new and passionate. Leaving Thorn wasn't easy, and I don't want people to think that it was. I still want him to be in my life...because I can't live without him."

Even I was moved by her interview, and I already knew all of this. Titan was speaking from the heart, pleading directly to Thorn. She didn't care about Denise or the rest of the world. This was her last attempt to get Thorn back, to take the media's hatred and relieve it from his shoulders. She spoke so highly of him, made it seem like she was the one missing out on something wonderful. It was a good tactic, and she pulled it off well.

Thorn would have to be made of stone not to care.

WHEN I STOPPED BY THORN'S OFFICE, I BYPASSED HIS assistant altogether and pushed through the doors. It happened so quickly that his assistant didn't realize what had happened until my body had crossed the threshold.

Thorn was on the phone when I stepped inside, and his eyebrows immediately jumped to the top of his forehead when he saw me barge in. "Steve, let me

call you back. A shithead just walked into my office."
He hung up and continued to stare at me
aggressively.

"Did you see it?"

Thorn stayed behind his desk, his shoulders
hunched with tension.

"I'll take that as a yes." I didn't help myself to a
seat. Instead, I stood directly in front of his desk,
invading his space like I had every right to do so.

Thorn continued to watch me from behind his
stoic mask. Something filled the air between us, a
gentle hostility.

I didn't understand why he kept his silence over
this. He had to say something.

He finally spoke. "Yes. I saw it."

Judging by his cold demeanor, it didn't move him
the way it moved me. "Then why are you on the
phone with Steve instead of Titan? She's earned
your forgiveness, so you need to give it to her. Call
her." I thudded my fist against the surface of
his desk.

"I would much rather look like an asshole than
some pussy shit who got left for another man. If you
ask me, I look worse."

"Then think again, Thorn. From what I saw, she
made you look amazing. She said a lot of wonderful

things about you, and she said she only left because she found the person she was meant to be with. It doesn't make any of us look bad."

He rested his fingertips against his temple.

"When the headlines start rolling in, you'll see. And then you better give Titan what she deserves."

"What?"

"Forgiveness."

7

TITAN

I SUCCESSFULLY DIRECTED the rage away from Thorn, providing a very different outlook on the breakup. I came clean about my love for Diesel, confessing to the world that he was the man I wanted for the rest of my life. A weight had lifted off my shoulders, but a new stress had swept over me at the same time.

There was no going back now.

Our privacy was something I greatly valued. I loved being together without anyone knowing about it. It made it much more intimate, much more special. Now cameras would be in our faces all of the time, and our relationship would be a spectacle that tabloids would constantly comment on. There would always be rumors, always be lies.

But I knew Diesel hated the secrecy, and it would

be wrong to continue to hide him. I certainly wasn't ashamed of him, so I needed to stop acting like it.

My eyes kept drifting back to the phone on my coffee table, hoping it would ring. I hoped I would see Thorn's name on the screen. But that call never came. The screen remained black, and I continued to sit in the dark as I waited for Diesel to walk inside.

A moment later, he did.

He stepped inside my penthouse in the suit he wore to work, skipping the gym and heading straight for my place. That was an admission of knowledge, that he knew about the interview I gave earlier that afternoon. He obviously wasn't happy about it. Otherwise, he would have mentioned it sooner.

"Hi." I rose to my feet, my heels gone, so I was back to being five inches shorter than I usually was.

He stripped off his coat and left it by the door. "Did you see the reporters outside?"

"That was all I could see."

He walked toward me, a powerful man in a powerful suit. His suit was just as crisp as it had been when he put it on that morning. He always looked good in black, but then again, he looked good in every other color too.

He walked up to me then angled his neck down so he could look into my face. There wasn't anger in his look, but there wasn't happiness either. His hands moved to my waist, and his fingers dug into me tightly, touching me possessively even though he hadn't kissed me yet. "Did you mean what you said?"

My eyes moved to his lips, seeing the stubble along his jaw.

"That I'm your soul mate?"

My arms rested on his, and I looked at his chest, seeing the silk tie that covered the buttons of his shirt. "I can't think of anyone else I would sacrifice so much for..." My fingers felt his biceps through the fabric, my eyes still on his chest.

His hand moved to my neck, and he tilted my face up so I was forced to meet his gaze.

"Loving you has gone against my better judgment. My love is more powerful than reason, more crazy than it is sane. The second you walked into my life, everything has been different. I've changed all my priorities to accommodate you, broken rules I vowed never to break. The only man I would ever do that for is the love of my life...and that's you."

His thumb sat in the corner of my mouth, and he watched me with an intense expression. He didn't crack a smile, but he smothered me with his gaze. His hand tightened on my hip, and he shifted his body closer to mine. "And you're mine." He leaned in and kissed the corner of my mouth, his touch warm and erotic. His lips trailed down my cheek then along my jawline toward my ear. He kissed the shell before he spoke. "I knew the moment I laid eyes on you." He wrapped his arms around my waist and pulled me against his chest. His chin rested on my head, and his large arms encompassed most of my back. I felt like I was being squeezed by a python as well as a strong man.

My face rested against his broad chest. "I'm surprised you aren't mad at me."

"I was. But what's done is done."

"I was going to tell you... I just never got around to it. And then when I saw Thorn..."

"I understand."

"But he hasn't called. I know he saw it."

His arm moved up the center of my shoulder blades, and he gently caressed my hair. "He'll come around."

"I don't know. I thought he would call by now."

"He's probably just digesting everything. Once he sees the aftermath of what you did, he'll be back."

"I hope so." I stepped back from his embrace so I could look at his face. I found comfort in the hardness of his features, the masculine edges that made him handsome and slightly terrifying. "I'm really happy with what we have. But I'm constantly held back by my sorrow. It's like a pain in my stomach that just won't go away."

Diesel had been understanding of Thorn from the very beginning. He was never threatened by my relationship with him, and he wanted us to keep our special friendship. Anyone else wouldn't have tolerated it. "I know, baby. I really believe it'll work out. You just need to be patient a little longer."

I gave a slight nod, falling into that reassurance. I'd just told the world that I was the reason Thorn and I weren't together. Some people would take the news with an open mind, but some would call me a two-timing whore. Some would turn their backs on me, and others would publish hateful articles about my character and demeanor. People would question my business ethics next. When it came to women, everything else about their life was brought into question. But if I were a man, no one would think twice about it. I was willing to accept the punishment directed my way, but I just hoped it wasn't all in vain.

All I wanted was my friend back.

Diesel continued to stare into my face, watching me with concern and intensity. "I'm sorry you had to do this, but I would be lying if I said I wasn't happy that the world knows about the two of us."

That was all he'd wanted, for a long time. "I know."

"I know the guys are going to be mad...but they'll get over it. I've accomplished a lot of things in my life, things I'm immensely proud of. But I have to say, I've never been more proud of anything than you. Tatum Titan told the whole world that she loves me... I'm such a lucky man."

My hands slid up his chest, my mouth forming a soft smile. "Because I'm a notch on your belt?"

"No." His hands squeezed my hips. "Because you erased all my old notches."

NEITHER ONE OF US THOUGHT ABOUT DINNER, AND WE spent our time in bed. We made love a few times, climaxing together and soaking the sheets with the aroma of sex. I was on top for one round, but he quickly took over for the next.

Then we lay side by side, cuddled together and relaxed in our mutual silence. My fingers moved over the grooves of his chest and shoulders, and I didn't think about the world outside my penthouse.

Undoubtedly, every news station mentioned the live interview I gave that afternoon. People were dissecting it, breaking it down over and over again. Reporters must have reached out to Thorn and his team for a comment on the story. Knowing him, he declined.

Diesel only had eyes for me. He could have stared at the ceiling or the sheets, but his eyes remained focused on me. His large hands explored my body like he hadn't just touched me everywhere for the past hour. His rough fingertips glided against my hips and around my waist. "Beautiful."

"You always say that."

"Because I mean it." His voice was deep and scruffy, rough like the hair around his jaw. His eyes were unremarkable in appearance, not bright and rare the way Thorn's were, but they suited him perfectly. Their deep color, their powerful vibrancy, ideally matched the man who wore them.

"I think you're beautiful."

He grinned. "Well, obviously."

I chuckled then lightly swatted him on the arm. "I do."

"I know, baby." His hand slid to my stomach, where he gripped my waistline and the small abs that existed just below my skin. "I had lunch with my father today."

I hadn't expected Vincent and Diesel to speak for a while. They'd had a good conversation, but I'd expected it to be months before Diesel would see him in a setting like that. "You did?" I should have wiped my smile away, but I couldn't.

"Yeah. He stopped by my office and asked me to go."

"That's nice."

"At first, I said no. I didn't want to do something so normal when we were anything but normal. But then I felt guilty for turning him down. He didn't show his disappointment, but I could tell he was hoping for more. So I said yes..."

"And how was it?"

"Awkward and uncomfortable."

My smile fell. "It's not going to be easy in the beginning."

"We stuck to discussions about business. That made it a little easier."

"Baby steps."

"And then he mentioned your plan to tell the media about your relationship with Thorn." He flashed me a look full of accusation. "I was caught off guard because it surprised me that you would tell my father something like that before you told me."

He didn't paint me in a good light. Made it seem like I was purposely hiding the news from him. "I was having a bad day when he called. So we got to talking, and I asked for his advice. He was actually the one who suggested it."

His gaze darkened.

"I liked the idea, so I considered it for a while. But I wasn't going to say anything to you until I made a decision."

"And then what happened?" he asked. "Because I never got a phone call."

"I saw Thorn in that restaurant...and I just went for it. I was upset and emotional. I just want this pain to stop. I know it was stupid and could do more harm than good, but I had to do something. If it works, then I'll have no regrets. And if it doesn't work...at least I'll know I tried."

His anger washed away, and his hand caressed me. "It'll work, baby."

"I'm sorry I didn't tell you first."

"It's okay. I was just surprised you told my father first."

"I didn't plan on it. But he's actually a very easy person to talk to. He asked me a few things, and before I knew it, I was telling him everything about Thorn and me." Diesel painted his father as an evil man, someone who didn't have a soul. But Vincent had treated me better than most men ever had, even before he knew I was seeing his son. I felt like an equal to him, someone he respected. I never took for granted those kinds of relationships because they were so rare. Thorn was one of the few who never thought twice about having women in positions of power. A lot of the high-ranking employees in his company were women.

"My father and I never really had conversations like that. We stuck to money, business, or my education. That's about it."

"Maybe things will be different now."

He stared into my eyes for a long time. "Maybe."

I understood Diesel was still hesitant to let his father back into his heart. I couldn't blame him, not after the things Vincent had done. His wrongful behavior came from pain, but it didn't excuse the lengths he was willing to go to to hurt Diesel. "So, I've been thinking."

"You're always thinking."

"Since you aren't the person who betrayed me, that means someone else did. We should figure out who that person is. If they really have a vendetta against me, I don't want them to sneak up on me when I'm not looking." I spent most of my time looking over my shoulder. As a woman with a lot of power, there were always people trying to take it away from me. I made enemies with people I'd never even met. Some people didn't find my success just intimidating, but wrong.

Diesel's expression changed into a look I'd never seen before. His mouth formed a partial smile, and his eyes lit up in a special way. His fingers kneaded the soft skin of my waist a little harder than before. "It means the world to me to hear you say that."

I never got the evidence I needed to clear Diesel's name, but I refused to believe a man who loved me so much would ever hurt me. He always had my back, even when I didn't know it, and he'd been loyal to me since the beginning. Maybe Thorn thought I was being stupid, but I was willing to gamble on Diesel. "I'm sorry I didn't believe you sooner."

"Don't apologize for that," he whispered. "It's over. I just want you to know it means a lot to me. That's all." He moved his face against mine on the pillow and kissed the corner of my mouth, his scruff rubbing against my soft skin. It was a slow kiss, sensual and deep like all the others, but it was filled with even more meaning. He pulled away a moment later, his eyes still filled with the same look of love.

I enjoyed the sight of his handsome face for another moment before I spoke. "Who do you think it is?"

He released a quiet sigh. "I'm not sure, baby. With Thorn—"

"It's not him." I didn't believe in a lot of things, but Thorn was something I believed in deeply. There was no doubt in my mind that he would never betray me. Even now, he still wouldn't hurt me.

Diesel didn't push it. "That leads me back to Bruce Carol."

"He didn't act guilty. And if he did all those things, I don't know why he wouldn't gloat."

"Me neither," he said. "Unless there's another stage to his plan..."

I hoped not. I finally had Diesel publicly, and I was on the road to happiness. I didn't want to be attacked again. "What about Vincent?"

Diesel didn't reject it right away. "I've been wondering that too. He's been watching both of us for a long time, and we've both seen exactly what he's capable of."

I admit Vincent did some terrible things, but that seemed unlikely. "I don't think he would do that."

"I don't know...he did blackmail me."

"But he also didn't go through with it."

"Because you told him not to," he countered.

"I doubt he would have done it even if I hadn't."

"No way for us to know. I know you want my father and me to work things out, but let's not rewrite history. He's capable of terrible things because he's done terrible things."

I wanted to believe Vincent was a better man than he made himself seem, but I knew that would be naïve. "Then let's ask him."

"Outright?"

"Yes. Maybe he did do it. But I don't think he'd lie about it."

Diesel considered it in silence, his eyes shifting back and forth as he looked into mine. "You're right. He wouldn't lie." He seemed to be reliving a memory behind his eyes. "That was something he always said to me. A man doesn't lie about the things he's done. He admits them openly and faces the consequences."

"Then I guess we'll start there."

I checked the headlines that afternoon

Diesel Hunt and Tatum Titan—Soul Mates?

Titan Followed Her Heart to True Happiness.

Tatum Titan—Lying Two-Timer?

Thorn Cutler Is the Man Of Her Dreams, Just Not Her Soul Mate.

I skimmed through a dozen more and was pleased to see the overall reaction. A few people said some harsh things about my character, but it didn't hurt because I'd been anticipating that. Most people concentrated on the fact that I'd fallen in love with the person I was meant to be with, and I didn't have any other choice but to do what I did. They seemed to be understanding, and most importantly, Thorn came out looking good rather than bad. I did my best to make sure it seemed like I was the one losing out on him, not the other way around.

Jessica spoke through the phone. "I have Vincent Hunt on line one."

"Thanks." I picked up the phone and took the call without thinking twice about it. Vincent had become a part of my life overnight. Now I didn't hesitate whenever he was on the line. "Hey, Vincent."

"Hello, Titan. I've been reading the tabloids today, something I never do. You did a great job."

"Thanks...it seems to be working."

"That wasn't easy to do. You controlled the narrative and manipulated the media into reporting a specific version of the story you told. Impressive."

I chuckled. "Well, I've been the subject of the media for a long time..."

"And you handle it gracefully," he said with a deep voice, a tone similar to Diesel's. "Has Thorn reached out to you?"

I hated giving this answer. I hated staring at my phone all day as I waited for him to call. I hated this separation between us, terrified that there was nothing I could do to get my friend back. "No."

Vincent was quiet for a long time, his silence stretching over the phone. "I'm sorry to hear that. But it's only been one day."

"Yeah..."

Vincent sat on the phone with me, letting the silence stretch between us.

There were very few people I could just sit on the phone with. Diesel and Thorn were the other two. "Diesel and I wanted to ask you something. Are you free tonight?"

"No, but I can be free."

"You don't need to rearrange your plans—"

"There's nothing I'd rather be doing than spending time with my son." He cut me off with his strong voice, laying down the law so effortlessly, it was no surprise he was one of the biggest suits in the world. "Just tell me when and where."

"How about my place after work?"

"I'll be there."

"May I ask what your plans were?" I'd never ask anyone else a personal question like that, but I felt like I could. Vincent knew most of the intimate details of my life to a high degree.

He didn't say anything for a while. "Dinner with a woman I'm seeing."

I'd seen him with a few different women at events or in the papers, but I'd never given his personal life much thought before. Every woman he had on his arm was gorgeous and half his age. But he had a special kind of handsomeness that had followed him throughout life. I knew he could get those women not just because he was rich, but because he was exceptionally good-looking. "I'd tell you to bring her along, but the conversation is private."

"I wouldn't bring her around anyway. We aren't serious." Just like his son, he was the kind of man that didn't commit.

I didn't ask any more questions. "I'll see you then."

By evening, I still hadn't heard from Thorn.

Maybe he would never call.

What more did he have to think about? I put myself on the line and risked humiliating myself to the entire world. That didn't mean anything to him? My sadness was starting to escalate into anger. Thorn had every right to be mad about the things that I did, but he shouldn't stay angry forever.

Diesel stepped out of the elevator in his gray suit and black tie. Even though the penthouse was mine, he owned it every single time he was in the space. His silent intensity, his strong presence always filled every single inch of the place.

I got up to meet him, trying to swallow the sadness I felt about Thorn.

But there was no hiding from Diesel. With just one look, he could read every expression on my face. His hand dug into my hair, and he kissed me in the living room, his strong mouth caressing mine.

My arms circled his neck, and I let my fingers explore his short hair. He smelled like cologne and scotch, obviously having had a few drinks during the day. He'd shaved that morning so I felt his smooth skin against my mouth. He was warm and hard, a man made of solid muscle and bones of steel.

His hands slid to my waist, and he rested them on the curve of my back. "Don't lose hope."

"I'll try."

He kissed my temple before he released me. "Do I have time to shower?"

"He'll be here any minute." Just when I finished the sentence, the elevator beeped. "Looks like he's here."

The doors opened a moment later, and Vincent stepped out in a navy blue suit with a black tie. He had the same threatening expression in his eyes even when his intent was to be friendly. He stepped inside and greeted us both with a look. He still hadn't shaken Diesel's hand or extended any other kind of affection, probably knowing it was too soon.

"Can I get you something to drink, Vincent?"

"No, thank you." He turned his eyes on his son, the person in the room he cared most about.

Diesel wore a similar expression to his father's, meeting his gaze with the same silent strength. It seemed to be a family trait—that confident stare. His hands moved into his pockets, dismissing any kind of physical greeting. Diesel remained on edge, always tense whenever his father was in the same room. As if that lunch had never happened, they were still worlds apart.

I ushered the men into the living room. "Let's have a seat." If I didn't break their trance, there was no way to know how long they would stare at each other. We moved to the couch, Diesel and me on one while Vincent took the other.

That heavy silence stretched out again.

I cleared my throat before I spoke. "Diesel and I wanted to ask you something."

Vincent rested his elbows on his knees and brought his hands together. "I'm listening."

"A few months ago, someone leaked that story about me to the papers."

Vincent nodded. "I remember."

"The newspaper claimed Diesel was the source, but Diesel denies it."

Vincent nodded again. "I know. I read it."

"Well, it wasn't Diesel," I said. "We think someone tried to frame him. We aren't sure who did it, and we aren't certain why either."

Vincent's gaze slowly shifted back and forth between the two of us. He examined me like a specimen under a microscope, and then he turned his attention back to his son, watching him with the same intense scrutiny. "You think it was me."

"No," I said quickly. "We're asking if it was you."

Diesel rested his hand on my thigh, his affection natural even when we weren't alone. "Was it?"

Vincent's expression didn't change. He didn't seem angered by the question. In fact, he didn't have any real reaction at all. "No. I want to feel offended by the accusation, but I know I have no right to be."

That was enough for me. I believed Vincent would come clean if he had been the perpetrator.

Diesel didn't ask any more questions either.

"You're a powerful woman, Titan," Vincent said. "They say it's lonely at the top because it is. You've built an empire entirely on your own, and no matter what obstacles get in your way, you still carry on with your head held high. Of course, people will be jealous. Of course, they'll want to tear you down. That's probably the reason why, simple as that. In regards to who's behind it...that's not as simple."

I suspected I would never get to the bottom of this. I could have an archnemesis working alongside me every day. Perhaps it was an old vendor, a previous client...I didn't know. All I knew was that it wasn't Diesel—and it wasn't Vincent.

Vincent continued. "This person probably fulfilled their desire when they published that story about you. They got what they wanted and moved on with their life. There's a good possibility it's over. You don't need to look over your shoulder anymore. Your reputation has remained intact despite all the roadblocks."

"Or they aren't finished," Diesel added. "And we'll always be looking over our shoulders for the next attack."

Everyone had an enemy. No one was unanimously liked by every person they met throughout their life. There were always potholes along the road.

Vincent rubbed his large hands together. "I can help. Keeps my eyes and ears open. Do you have any suspects?"

"Bruce Carol," Diesel said. "Titan and I both competed for his company when it was going under. He said some pretty offensive things about Titan, so I bowed out of the deal. Titan purchased the company for a fraction of what I offered, and it wasn't enough to cover all of his debts, so he essentially lost everything."

Vincent stopped rubbing his hands together, his eyes focusing on Diesel. "I think you have your culprit right there."

"I confronted him," Diesel continued. "He denied it."

"Doesn't matter if he denied it," Vincent said. "Of course, he's going to lie out of his ass. That's what weasels like him do." He lowered his hands then straightened his posture. "Anyone else come to mind?"

"No," I said. "Diesel thought it was Thorn, but that's impossible."

"You're certain?" Vincent pressed.

It was stupid for me to have suspected him in the first place. "Absolutely."

"Then Bruce is your man," Vincent said. "When a man hits rock bottom, there's no telling what he'll do. I've heard he's a sexual harassment lawsuit waiting to happen, so it doesn't surprise me one bit."

"What did you hear?" I wasn't ignorant of the inappropriate events that took place in the business world. When wealthy men had power and friends in high places, they thought they were invincible. They abused their power by forcing women to do what-ever they wanted or face the professional conse-quences. I'd been touched inappropriately in the office before, and I didn't feel any remorse when I sprained a few ankles and knees. No one could pull stunts like that with me. Once I became the richest woman in the world, men didn't think about crossing me anymore.

Vincent answered simply. "Threatens to fire women if they don't give him what they want. For interviews for assistant positions, he has them meet him at a hotel where he conducts the interview in his hotel room. He offers them a great paycheck with benefits, but says they have to convince him to hire them...very shady stuff."

That man really was vile. I felt terrible for his wife and children. I didn't blame them for leaving.

"Fits the description perfectly," Diesel said. "I guess I'll keep him on my radar. Last I heard, his penthouse had been seized by the banks and he was leaving the city. Not sure where he's going or if he has offshore accounts somewhere."

"Every wealthy person does," Vincent said. "I have an idea."

"What?" I asked.

"I've met with Bruce a few times. We haven't done business together extensively, but we know each other well enough. He's aware that Diesel and I haven't spoken in a decade. It's come up in conversation before. I could arrange a meeting with him and determine his feelings toward Titan." His eyes shifted to me. "I could say some terrible things and see if he confesses. You can't take legal action against a man who doesn't have anything, at least, if it's not a criminal case. But at least you would have your answer."

Vincent Hunt was busier than most, but he lived off the radar. His name was well-known, and his businesses were huge, but he stayed out of the tabloids. He led a quiet life out of the public eye. For him to get involved in this was generous. "You'd do that?"

He held my gaze with the same confidence Diesel always showed. "Anything I can do to help."

"He might know it's a setup," Diesel said.

"And if he realizes it is, I don't care," Vincent said. "No harm done."

"I don't want him to have a vendetta against you as well," I countered.

"I'm untouchable." He leaned back against the couch and rested his arm over the back. "I have security with me at all times, even if they can't be seen. The penthouse directly across from mine is staffed with a team that does surveillance for my private use. I'm not worried about a broke man who was too proud to save his business when he had the chance." He leaned forward again, adjusting his cuff links. "We have a plan?"

Diesel considered it before he gave a nod. "Yeah. We have a plan."

8

THORN

THE MEDIA GOT off my back.

As if they'd never been interested in me in the first place, they disappeared.

But my mom kept calling me—over and over.

I pitied her because everything happened so fast. One moment, her oldest son was getting married to the finest woman in the world. And then everything changed. Her son was painted as a jerk and a heart-breaker. I thought about telling her the truth, but I thought that would just make her more upset.

From what I read in the tabloids, it seemed like people had responded to Titan's manipulation. She'd put her reputation on the line when she pulled that stunt. The narrative could have gone quite differently, but she managed to control a situation that was out of her control.

She never ceased to impress me.

Her intention was bluntly obvious. It was her last attempt to make amends with me, to earn my forgiveness after she betrayed me and fed me to the wolves. She was willing to look like the fool so I could walk away unscathed.

I'd be lying if I said it didn't mean something to me.

She'd called me a few times, but I never answered. Every time I let those calls go to voice mail, I felt the pain rise in my chest. My hand ached to take the call, but my stubbornness always steadied it.

I missed her.

I missed us.

But I still hadn't reached out to her, unsure exactly what I wanted. Distance had made my heart grow fonder, and my stubbornness only lasted so long. Now I wanted what we lost. I wanted that unbreakable loyalty we used to have. I never flinched when I had her back. She didn't flinch when she had mine.

I wasn't heartless, and I understood the predicament she was in. Falling in love had clouded her judgment in a way I'd never seen before. Titan wasn't relying on that enormous brain of hers anymore. She was thinking with her heart—for once. Whether Diesel was the right choice or not, I understood her decision. In any other situation, I would have respected it.

But not after she betrayed me.

Only now my focus had been strained. I found myself wanting to call her to share news with her. I found myself missing the person I used to share my life with. I confided everything in her, showed her my true colors because I knew I would be accepted for exactly who I was. There wasn't a single thing I could say that would make her look at me differently. That was true friendship, true loyalty.

I would never find that again.

So maybe I should end the war and pick up the damn phone.

"Sir?" My assistant spoke through the intercom. "Mr. Vincent Hunt is here to see you."

Vincent Hunt? Diesel's father? I'd never spoken directly to Vincent, but I knew exactly who he was— and not just because of his relation to Diesel. He was a gladiator of the corporate world, building an empire that intimidated everyone. He brought a new definition to the word successful. I also knew how vicious he was. According to Titan, he didn't restrain from doing evil things—even to his own son.

"Sir?"

Taken aback by her announcement, I forgot to respond. "Send him in." I wasn't doing anything productive anyway, and I was curious to know what this man wanted. He went to Titan to turn her against Diesel. Perhaps that's why he was there now —to turn me against both Titan and Diesel.

I already knew I couldn't take any deal he offered. I couldn't betray Titan...no matter how good the deal was. No matter what she did to me, I would always remain loyal to her. She was a good person with a bigger heart than she cared to admit. She would never hurt me on purpose—and I knew that.

Vincent Hunt walked in a moment later, looking even bigger in my office than he did from across the room. In a crisp suit custom made just for him, he walked to the chair facing my desk, his intimidating stare directed on me. He bypassed a handshake and took a seat. His beefy size reminded me of Diesel's musculature. They were both large men, and I was on the leaner, ripped side of the spectrum.

I held his gaze, unflinching.

He did the same to me.

The stare lasted for a while, neither one of us speaking first.

Finally, he said something. "I don't believe we've met."

"Not in person, but your reputation precedes you." That included the good as well as the bad. From what Titan described, he seemed to be a dictator with serious control issues. If he felt slighted, he wouldn't stop until he got his revenge. He was petty, spiteful.

He crossed his legs and placed his large arms on the armrests of the chair, looking imposing as he took up most of the chair. For a middle-aged man, he looked as healthy as a horse. He retained his physique as time enhanced his beauty, and he appeared to be fifteen years younger than he truly was. That was how I hoped to look when I reached his age.

Vincent took another long pause before he spoke again. Silence didn't affect him.

Didn't affect me either.

"I've gotten to know Titan recently, and she's a very impressive woman. You don't know me, but that's a bold statement for me to make. You see, nothing impresses me anymore. I've seen it all, heard it all. But she has something the rest of us lack. She's scrappy, gritty, but elegant at the same time. You're a lucky man to have such a big piece of her heart. I know her love isn't romantic because I see the way she looks at my son, but that doesn't make it less powerful. You're sitting on your ass doing nothing when you could be spending your time in a much better way. That doesn't impress me."

I'd expected to be pitched, but instead, I got a lecture. This was the first time I'd ever met this man face-to-face, and he gave me his two cents on a matter he knew nothing about. It was bold, but it was also effective.

"I made the mistake of holding on to my anger for the past ten years. I banished my son from my life when I could have fixed the issue instead. Now I'm groveling on my knees trying to earn his trust again. If I could go back in time, I would have done things much differently. I wish I could get back all that time that I lost. Instead, I held on to my stubbornness and pride. Look where that got me." He tilted his head slightly as he focused his gaze on my face. He stared at me like he could see me through me despite the fact that I was a solid wall of man. "Don't make the same mistake I did. Titan has done everything she can to earn your forgiveness. She's out of ideas. Now it's up to you. You can do nothing and let time pass until a decade of silence has gone by, or you can get your friend back." He rose from the chair as if the conversation was over. He walked to the door. "It was nice meeting you, Thorn. I hope we meet again...under better circumstances."

9

DIESEL

THE ANNUAL BUSINESS Leaders of America gala was tonight, and I received an invitation, as did Titan. It was an evening meant for the businesses stationed in New York City. The mayor was usually there, along with the senators. Last year, the president of the United States stopped by for a visit. Donations went to the city, helping homeless shelters, after-school programs, and public transportation systems.

My father was the keynote speaker tonight.

I knew the paparazzi would be following Titan and me closely. It was our first public appearance as a couple. It would be the perfect opportunity to photograph us together. Any other worldwide news would come second to our romance.

I stood in the living room and adjusted my solid black watch. I was in a black suit and tie, choosing a darker look since Titan was wearing a black dress. I didn't try to match her, but I also wanted our appearances to complement each other.

My driver was waiting downstairs at the curb, and we were running late.

Titan finally stepped out of the bedroom in a black cocktail dress with a slight shimmer in the fabric. She was in sky-high heels, and the dress featured a strapless sweetheart top. Her brown hair trailed down her chest in curls.

I let out a soft whistle.

Despite how confident she was, she smiled and allowed a light hint of blush to fill her cheeks. "You're sweet." She grabbed her clutch off the table, a matching black wallet that had a subtle hint of glitter to it.

My arms immediately encircled her waist, and I pressed my face closer to hers. "I'm not trying to be sweet."

"Seems that way." Her hands slowly migrated up my chest, feeling the hardness underneath my collared shirt. She touched me with soft aggression, her fingertips pressing into me like she wanted to feel my bare skin.

My hands slid down her ass, skimming the soft fabric until I reached the tops of her thighs. I pulled the fabric, moving it upward until I revealed her sexy ass in just her black thong. My fingers gripped the gorgeous muscles of her perky ass. Time didn't seem important to me anymore. I was hard in my slacks, and there was no way I could last all night without having her at least once now. I slowly backed her up toward the dining table.

She held her ground and stopped me. "No. We're running late."

"Don't care." My hand moved underneath the fall of her hair, and I kissed her, knowing my lips would silence her protests. My mouth had a natural way of getting what it wanted. I knew how to kiss her the way she liked, how to take her breath away with a simple touch. She did the same thing to me, bringing my passion to the surface until it couldn't be controlled.

Her lipstick smeared across my mouth as she sucked my bottom lip. Her tongue delved into my mouth, exploring me as if she'd never kissed me before. With anxious hands and unsteady breath, she couldn't hide her desire for me. She could be in a hurry to leave one moment, and then almost immediately forget what we were dressed up for in the first place.

My hands guided her to the table, and once

her back hit the wood, I pulled her thong to her thighs. She hopped on the table just as I lifted her, and then I pulled her thong down her beautiful legs until it hit the floor. She gripped my shoulders as she kissed me, and I undid my belt and slacks so I could get my cock free. My boxers were pushed down over my ass, and my throbbing dick was released and ready for her delectable pussy.

She lay back and propped herself on her elbows so she wouldn't ruin her hair, and I pulled her hips to the very edge before I shoved myself inside her. I moved completely within her, feeling her tight walls surround me and seal me inside. She was wet, warm, and tight. Like I'd never been inside her before, I paused to enjoy her.

With my eyes locked on hers, I pinned my arms behind her knees and started to move. Time wasn't on our side, but that didn't make me fuck her faster. I took it slow, rocking into her with deep and even strokes.

Her tits shook, her nipples hardened, and she parted her sexy lips as she moaned for me.

She hooked one arm around my neck and held herself up with her other hand. She widened her legs farther, bit her bottom lip as her entire body shook with my thrusts, and stared at me with sexy, fearless eyes.

Now I just wanted to stay home with her.

"Diesel..." No other woman had ever said my name in such a sexy way. She could do it so easily, so powerfully. Her lips opened more as her moans deepened and increased in volume.

I moved my mouth to hers and kissed her as I made love to her on the dining table, worshiping the only woman I'd ever loved. She was the only woman I'd been this intimate with, the only one I removed a condom for. She was the only woman who commanded my respect so easily. She was the only woman who brought me to my knees. Only a woman like Tatum Titan could make a man out of me.

Her nails dug into the back of my neck as she moved with me on the table. Her breathing quickened, her gasps filling my mouth. Her body slowly tightened around me, unexpected moans emerging. "I love you..." She came around me the second the words were out of her mouth, a beautiful confession that made my entire body shake.

I came seconds afterward, filling her pussy at the exact moment it squeezed my hard dick. My possessiveness for her increased every time I released inside her, wanting her to be mine and no one else's.

I was the only man on this planet good enough for her, strong enough to handle a woman so independent and successful. Even if she passed me on the Forbes list, all I would feel was pride. I found her brains sexy, her powerful demeanor thrilling. Only a man as successful and secure as I was could handle such an amazing woman.

I stayed inside her even when I was finished, loving the feeling between her legs. It felt so good, so perfect. I wanted to stay buried inside her forever, to feel my own come push past my shaft and back out her entrance. I rubbed my nose against hers as the breath left my lungs. "I love you too."

Her fingers dug into the back of my hair, and she pressed a soft kiss to my lips. "I can tell."

I had just given her an impressive mound of come, and it was already dripping from her body onto the table. It didn't matter how many times I'd already had her, my body was always so eager that it gave her everything it had—every time.

JUST AS I ANTICIPATED, THE PHOTOGRAPHERS WERE lined up at the doorway to the hotel the second we alighted from of the car. I stepped out first and extended my hand to Titan.

She rose with perfect posture, a cheeky smile on her lips, and took my hand with a strong grip.

I was immobilized by the image, seeing this queen step out for the cameras and grab my hand. She was there with me, showing the world I was the man she'd chosen. We'd been a secret for so long, sneaking around in hotel rooms abroad and throughout the city. Now there was no more hiding. The world recognized us as a couple—two people in love.

I couldn't remember a time when I was this happy.

I guided her through the entryway, holding her close to me and taking the lead. Flashes erupted in front of my face, the lights blinding. I never smiled for pictures. I usually didn't smile at all. But this time, I did.

Because I had a very special reason to smile.

When we made it inside, the flashes finally stopped. My hand moved around her slender waist, and I guided her to the ballroom where the dinner was being held. My heart was beating with the adrenaline rush that had just washed over me. I was excited in a way I'd never been before. I was about to walk into a room with all my colleagues, and they would know I was the lucky man who got to keep Titan to himself.

Titan stayed close to me, but she looked as independent and confident as she usually was. She was my date, but she was always her own person. Her eyes scanned the room before she turned her eyes on me. "I think I need a drink."

We entered the throng of people, and immediately, almost everyone was looking at us. They wanted to see our affection with their own eyes, see us together after Titan had confessed to the world that I was her soul mate.

During our conversations with friends and acquaintances, I kept my hand on her the entire time. If I could have, I would have made the affection even more extensive, giving her a kiss that wouldn't be appropriate for the room. But Titan wouldn't go for it, so I didn't push it.

We talked with the mayor for a few minutes then moved on to other people. The two of us stuck to the champagne the waiters were passing around even though both of us were more interested in scotch and whiskey.

When we finally had a minute alone, I spoke to

her quietly. "People seem fascinated by our relationship."

"Not surprised," she said before she took a drink. "I did just share my personal life with the entire world."

My hand rested on the small of her back. "I like it. After all the months of hiding and pretending, we don't have to lie anymore. Now I can stare at you all I want. I can touch you whenever I feel like it. And I can kiss you whenever I want." I slowly leaned in, watching the expression in her eyes intensify as I drew near. She didn't turn away or press a hand to my chest, so I moved in completely and gave her a soft kiss.

She kissed me back, her lids shutting momentarily.

Even though the embrace lasted only a few seconds, it was enough to shoot the excitement through me. I felt the tenderness at the edge of my fingertips, the heat in my chest. Only one woman could make me burn like this, and she was standing right in front of me.

When she leaned back, the same passion was in her eyes. She'd just made love to me before she left, and she could have another round if the situation permitted it. That was how our nights were spent—

not sleeping, only fucking. Every morning I was exhausted, but I wouldn't change anything about it.

"I'm the luckiest guy in this room." I spoke with my lips near her ear, my hand squeezing the fabric at her lower back.

A soft smile formed on her lips.

"I'm in love with the strongest woman in this room, and she's in love with me too. You can't put a price on that." The first time I kissed her, I knew there was something there. The first time we fucked, even then, I knew something was there. It took me a while to understand it, a few months to process it, but I recognized the love once I allowed myself to see it. Now it was right in front of me, staring bluntly back at me.

"I wouldn't say I'm the luckiest woman in the room...because every woman here hates me for having you."

I rubbed my nose against hers. "But you don't care, do you?"

Her smile widened. "No. I don't."

I kissed her temple before I pulled her with me, directing her to the next group of people to see. These functions were always about small talk, and right now, we needed to stop by and speak to Kyle Livingston next.

But then Thorn emerged from the left and magically appeared in front of us. In a navy blue suit with a cream collared shirt, he looked exactly the same as before. The color of the fabric brought out the bright intensity of his eyes, that ice-blue color that looked nothing like mine. His eyes were only on Titan, as if she were the only person in the room.

Titan's smile dropped as she stared into his expression, looking at her closest friend in the world. I could feel her sadness instantly infect the space around us. She was just happy a moment ago, but seeing Thorn immediately dragged her back into the depths of sorrow.

The people surrounding us turned our way, waiting to see what would happen between the two old alleged lovers.

I didn't know what to expect from Thorn. He looked angry, like Titan had somehow slighted him again. Maybe he wasn't happy about that interview, after all. Maybe it pissed him off even more. "Thorn, maybe we should talk about this later..." I stepped further into the situation, making sure some of my body blocked Titan. She didn't need me to protect her, but it was a natural urge I would never be able to combat.

"No." He still didn't look at me, his gaze reserved

for Titan. His eyes shifted slightly back and forth as he looked at her. His arms remained by his sides, but the tension started to unravel. It filled up the air between us, making all three of us tighten in preparation. The last time he'd seen Titan in a public place, he gave her the cold shoulder and walked off. Perhaps he was about to do that now, but to a more extreme degree. "I forgive you."

After reading the hostility in the room, I hadn't expected Thorn to say that. His emotions were compacted so tightly that they were difficult to read. I mistook his tension for anger.

Titan released the breath she was holding, the happiness immediately flooding into her eyes. I could see the wetness start to form, her eyes reflecting the lights from the chandeliers. "You do?"

Thorn nodded. "I miss you."

The tears welled up even more. "I miss you too." She left my embrace and moved into his chest, wrapping her arms around his neck and holding him tightly.

His large arms wrapped around her waist, and he squeezed her as he buried his face in her neck.

Instead of feeling jealous, all I felt was relief. I'd always thought Thorn would come to his senses and forgive Titan, but as his silence had lingered, that faith had slowly waned. But now that he was finally here with Titan, I knew the worst was over.

Now she was happy.

The embrace was longer than the others I'd seen. It seemed like Thorn needed it as much as Titan. These two friends had been there for each other through everything. Now everyone witnessed their reunion, and that would only make our story better.

Thorn was the first one to pull away, but he didn't have emotion in his face the way she did. He kept his features stoic, indifferent. He pulled his hand from her waist and placed both hands in his pockets.

I stared at them, trying to fade into the background so I could give them their space.

"Can we talk later?" Thorn asked quietly so no one could overhear them.

"Yeah. Come over."

"Alright." He turned to me next, still wearing the same expression. He stuck out his hand.

I shook it. "It's great to have you back."

He nodded. "It's great to be back."

AFTER DINNER, MY FATHER TOOK THE STAGE AND GAVE

his speech. Despite his greed for money and power, he did have philanthropic causes. I didn't know about most of them, but he'd been working on them for the last decade. He had been a lot quieter about his charitable donations—until now.

I think that had something to do with me.

Once dessert was finished, everyone returned to drinking and socializing. I was counting down the minutes until we could finally leave. Public appearances weren't as interesting anymore when there was only one place I wanted to be.

My father's immense figure parted the crowd as he came toward us. In a black tuxedo with slicked-back hair, he was the man of the hour. At his side was a woman Titan's age, a beauty with olive-toned skin and wearing a dark blue gown. She was a brunette, and she barely reached my father's shoulder even in her sky-high heels.

He reached for Titan first and shook her hand. "You look beautiful tonight, Titan."

"Thank you, Vincent," she said with a smile.

My father turned to me next. "Nice to see you, Diesel." He didn't extend his hand to me, forgoing the gesture and stepping back. He still hadn't tried to shake my hand, probably because he knew it was too soon for me to take it. "This is Alessia." He pronounced her name exotically, emphasizing the accent like he had a lot of practice saying her name. He didn't introduce her as anything else, such as a friend or girlfriend. He didn't touch her either, letting her stand beside him without an ounce of affection. "Alessia, this is my son, Diesel."

Alessia smiled before she took my hand. "It's nice to meet you. Your father talks about you a lot."

I didn't know what to say to that, so I nodded. "Nice to meet you too. You have a beautiful name."

"Thank you." She shook Titan's hand next. "I'm a fan of everything you do, Ms. Titan. You're an inspiration to all female entrepreneurs."

"Thank you," Titan said. "That's nice of you to say."

Alessia returned to my father's side, standing close to his shoulder. She had pronounced cheekbones, plump lips, lustrous eye makeup. She was exceptionally thin, looking like someone who counted her calories down to the last apple slice.

"What do you do?" Titan asked.

"She's a model," Vincent answered. "We met at a Milan fashion show a few months ago."

Alessia rubbed her hand up his arm. "We were introduced by a mutual friend. He's a gentleman, a lot more interesting than men my age." When she looked at my father, there was genuine affection in her eyes. She seemed to like him for him, not the billions in his bank account.

I'd seen my father with various women over the last decade. They were all half his age and beautiful. It didn't bother me to see him with someone else besides my mother. It was obvious they were just distractions, women to keep him occupied during his lonely nights. He didn't seem like the kind of guy who would get remarried, and based on the confessions he had made about my mother, he never wanted to.

But he kept his distance from Alessia, as if his being with a woman might offend me. "I saw you and Thorn talking." His eyes shifted back to Titan.

Titan lit up at the mention of him. "Yeah. We made up." She didn't say anything more than that with Alessia present.

"That's good to hear," my father said. "No reason why the two of you still can't be friends."

My arm circled Titan's waist, my hand gripping her opposite hip. She held herself perfectly straight, her shoulders back. I never slouched, but she made me even more aware of my own posture.

"Enjoy your night." My father dismissed us

before he turned away, Alessia moving with him like a small fish following an enormous shark.

"You too," Titan said.

My father walked away, joining a group of brokers from Wall Street.

Titan turned to me, her fingers immediately moving to the bottom of my tie. "I'm ready to go home."

"Me too."

"Then let's get out of here."

10

TITAN

W E RETURNED TO MY PENTHOUSE, and the second we were away from prying eyes, I slipped off my heels and tossed them across the room. I wore uncomfortable heels all day, every day, and I didn't want to wear them a second longer than I had to.

Diesel came up behind me. "Why don't you ever wear flats?"

"I don't like them."

He peeled off his jacket and draped it over the back of the couch. "I'm sure you'd be more comfortable, though."

"I don't care about comfort." Image was far more important. None of my skirts or dresses would look nearly as good if I weren't wearing a gorgeous pair of shoes. They showed off my calf muscles, made me a little taller, and gave me an extra jolt of attitude.

Diesel untied his tie and placed it on top of the jacket. He came to me next, his handsome face so gorgeous that I wanted to feel the chiseled lines of his jaw with my fingertips. "I had fun tonight— because I was with you."

"Me too."

His hands gripped my waist tightly, his thumb pressing over my ribs. "I'm glad things are okay with Thorn. I thought about it every day. I talked to him about it on multiple occasions. I'm glad he had a change of heart."

As if a slab of stone had been lifted from my chest, I could finally breathe easy again. Thorn was a constant in my life, and without him, I didn't know who I was anymore. He knew me when I was nothing, and he never changed his opinion of me even when I became something. He had always been genuinely happy for all of my successes. If anyone ever tried to tear me down, he had my back. He was family to me, the only person I had in the entire world. "You have no idea how much better I feel..."

At that same moment, the elevator beeped as it ascended to my floor.

It was Thorn.

Diesel released a quiet sigh before he pulled his

hands away. "I'll head back to my penthouse for the night. I'm sure you guys have a lot to talk about."

"You're more than welcome to stay, Diesel." He could stay as long as he wanted. He could stay in my bedroom and watch the game while Thorn and I talked in the living room. He'd been staying with me for so long it was hard for me to imagine him not being there.

"I know." He kissed me on the cheek. "But I'll give you guys some privacy. I should make sure my condo is still standing anyway. Someone could have robbed the place weeks ago, and I'd have no clue." He gave me a soft smile before he grabbed his jacket and tie from the couch.

We walked to the elevator and watched the doors open to reveal Thorn. Dressed in the same suit he'd worn to the gala, he stepped inside with his hands in his pockets. It wasn't quite the same as it used to be, the comfortable casualness we used to share. It was still tense, like our relationship hadn't reemerged just yet.

Diesel gave me another kiss before he stepped into the elevator. "Love you, baby."

My eyes met his. "I love you too." I watched him until the doors were shut and he was hidden from view. The second he was gone, a small weight returned to my chest. The idea of sleeping alone sounded unappealing. I was used to sharing everything with this man. A single night apart sounded like too much.

Silence stretched between us now that we were alone together. Thorn looked at me like he didn't know what to say. Not speaking for weeks had put a strain on our relationship that neither one of us could deny.

"Thanks for coming." I broke the silence and walked to the door. "Can I get you something?"

"My usual is fine." He moved to the couch and took a seat.

I came back with two glasses, a scotch for him and an Old Fashioned for me.

He took a long drink before he returned the glass to the table.

I sat on the other couch and held my glass between my fingers. "Thanks for coming."

"Of course," he said quietly. "Diesel didn't have to leave."

"He wanted to give us some privacy."

He stared down at his glass before he took another sip.

After another serving of silence, I started the conversation. "What made you change your mind?

Was it the interview?"

"It was part of it." He stared across the room toward the entryway, not making direct eye contact with me. "When I saw that interview, I was still mad. I was mad that the whole thing had happened. I still haven't spoken to my mom about it...don't know what to say to her."

I'd put a wedge between Thorn and his family, and that made me feel terrible. "I think you should just tell her the truth, Thorn. I can do it for you if you want. It would explain everything a lot more than the different versions she's seen on TV."

"Maybe," he said. "But I think it would hurt my parents to know I lied to them about something so big..."

"It's better than all the lies they're hearing now."

He bowed his head and gave a slight nod. "Yeah, I guess you're right."

"We can do it together. I don't mind. I don't want your parents to hate me. I love your parents."

"They could never hate you, Titan," he whispered. "They love you too."

His words swept over me, bringing a powerful sense of relief. I'd always considered them to be extended family. Losing them was just as hard as losing Thorn. Liv had always been like a mother to me. "Should we talk to them, then?"

"Yeah, I think so. I'll have to do it soon so they'll stop calling."

"How about tomorrow?" I asked.

He stared at the other side of the room as he considered it. "Yeah, that sounds good. They've been in town ever since we broke up publicly."

"Alright." I took a drink before I set the glass aside. "So, what changed your mind, if it wasn't that interview?"

Thorn stared at his hands as he rubbed them together. "Actually, it was Vincent Hunt."

That was the very last thing I expected him to say. I thought it could have been a dream, something Diesel said, or just his own misery. I didn't know Vincent had even spoken to him. "What?"

"He stopped by my office the other day and told me he regretted not speaking to Diesel for so long. He said he would do anything to get that time back. He'd held on to his pride and stubbornness far longer than he should have. He warned me not to make the same mistakes, not to throw away a friend-ship with a remarkable person. I guess those words went straight to my heart, made me think about my future without you in it. It made me sad...and that's when I knew I needed to let this go. Your decision hurt because of the impact it had on my life, but I do understand it. And of course, I forgive you. I should have let it go sooner than this." He finally turned his expression on me, his eyes remorseful. "I'm glad it's not too late."

"Thorn...it's never too late." I left my couch and took the seat right beside him. My arm hooked through his, and I rested my head on his shoulder, the scent of his cologne entering my nose. We had never been overly affectionate, but his touch was so nice. "I'm so glad you're back. I've been so lost without you. I'm happy with Diesel, but your absence left a pain in my stomach that I just couldn't get rid of."

"I was lost too."

"I never want to lose you again. This is for life."

"I know it is."

I lifted my head off his shoulder and looked at him. "I'm sorry it had to be this way. I really didn't know what else to do."

"It's okay," he said quietly. "I understand. Diesel is the man you want to spend the rest of your life with. You were put in a difficult position. No matter what choice you made, you lost someone."

I was grateful he was being so understanding.

"My interview really changed the narrative. I feel like people are sympathetic to both of us now. It didn't hurt your reputation or mine. I think everything is going to be fine."

"I think so too. You did a great job with that."

Because I didn't have any other choice. I had to get it right to save my friendship with Thorn.

"So...Diesel is the one?" He looked down at me with his blue eyes, no judgment present.

I nodded. "Yes...he is."

"You're going to marry him?"

We hadn't talked about it, but I knew it was coming. "Yes."

"And you're sure he didn't betray you?"

Even without any proof, I'd never been more certain of anything in my life. "Yes."

Thorn stared at me a few seconds longer before he turned away. "Then that's enough for me. If you believe him, then I believe him too."

"Thank you. Vincent, Diesel, and I have been talking about it. We think it's Bruce Carol. Vincent offered to help us get the information out of him."

"So, Vincent and Diesel are on good terms now?"

"Well...they're getting there." I hadn't told Thorn any of this because we hadn't been speaking. "Vincent has been trying to make things right with

Diesel. It's taken a while because of their history, but I know it'll happen eventually. It's hard for Diesel to trust him, and I can't say that I blame him."

"Neither can I." Thorn reached for my hand and held it. "I know we aren't going to be husband and wife. But that doesn't mean we can't spend our lives together."

"You're right."

He gave me a soft smile, his eyes full of emotions he never showed anyone else. "I guess I'll see you tomorrow, then." He rose from the couch and straightened his tie.

"Sure...unless you wanna hang out for a bit."

"You don't want to go after Diesel?"

"No. I can always do that later."

His smile widened. "Then I'd love to."

IT WAS OUR FIRST TIME SPENDING THE NIGHT APART, and after lying in bed and staring at the ceiling for an hour, I realized I wasn't going to get any sleep. I didn't want Diesel just because of the sex.

I wanted him for him.

I wanted to sleep on that hard chest and feel it rise and fall. I wanted to feel the warmth from his

large body as it filled the sheets. I wanted those
strong arms to wrap around me while I slept,
protecting me against everything in the cruel world.

I didn't want to sleep in this bed alone.

I finally got out of bed and pulled on a change of
clothes before I walked downstairs. My driver was
ready to go in ten minutes, so he took me down a few
blocks until I was outside Diesel's building. The
streets were fairly quiet for a Saturday night, so it
was unlikely anyone would see me. My hair was
pulled back and I didn't have any makeup on, but I
knew Diesel didn't care. Whether I looked my best
or my worst, he still saw me exactly the same way.

I hit the code in the elevator and rode it to the
top floor. The doors opened to his living room,
where only a few lights were on. He must have gone
to bed. I took off my shoes and left my jacket by the
door before I walked down the hallway.

His bedroom door was open, and all the lights
were lit. He lay there, the sheets bunched around his
waist. His hard chest was chiseled, even when he
was asleep.

I took off all my clothes except my panties and
crawled into bed beside him.

My weight shifted the bed, and it caused his eyes
to open. He looked at me, and after a second, he

recognized my face. A smile stretched on his lips, and those powerful arms wrapped around me the way I liked. "You couldn't make it one night?" he asked in his deep voice, heavy with testosterone and arrogance.

"I guess not."

He smiled and pulled me into his side. "Me neither."

———

I SAT BESIDE THORN IN THE RESTAURANT, MY LEGS crossed and my back perfectly straight. I hoped my photograph wouldn't be taken right now, especially when I would be joining Thorn and his parents. Hopefully, observers would see the situation for what it was—that I was still close to Thorn.

My nerves didn't usually get out of control like this. I was always calm and steady no matter the circumstances. But now my stomach couldn't settle, and I had the urge to jiggle my knee. I was about to tell my former almost in-laws that all of this had been a lie.

How could they possibly take that well?

"Nervous?" Thorn turned to me, one hand resting on the table.

"No. Why?"

"You look nervous."

"I don't look like anything."

He grinned. "Even when you wear a blank expression, I can tell when you're nervous."

"How?"

"Your eyebrows are slightly furrowed."

I forced myself to relax, and when I felt the tension release, I knew he was right.

He grinned wider. "Told ya."

I playfully slapped his arm and couldn't wipe the smile off my face. Our relationship seemed to be back to what it used to be. I was happy, I could actually cry.

"Go to Diesel's last night?"

"Yeah. I tried to sleep on my own, but I just lay there."

"You just lie there even when he's there," he teased.

I slapped his arm again. "I do not just *lie* there."

He chuckled. "Is that why you look so tired today?"

I shrugged, a smile on my face.

When Thorn smiled back, it seemed genuine. "What now? The world knows you're together, and the media seems to be responding to it well enough."

"He'll come back to Stratosphere. We made a great team."

"I don't mean professionally." Thorn came in a black t-shirt with dark jeans, looking like a different man when he was dressed casually. He was much softer when he wasn't in a suit, the veins on his arms more noticeable. He had the kind of boyish smile that melted the hearts of everyone around him. "Romantically."

"What's next?" I asked. "Happiness."

"I mean, are you still going to marry him?"

"I hope so."

"You haven't talked about it?"

"Not really." We spent most of our time just being together. Talking wasn't always included. We'd talked about getting married when we had our different arrangement, but now that it was just a real relationship, it wasn't so straightforward. "I think we should wait awhile so it doesn't look like I jumped from one engagement to the next, but if he asked, I'd say yes."

Thorn faced forward again when he saw his parents approach. "Here we go..."

Liv wasn't her usual bubbly self. She looked grief-stricken, like someone had died rather than just broken up. Thorn's father had a hard expression, looking pissed rather than hurt. Liv sat down, thudding into the chair like anchors were tied to her. "After all this time, I get a text message asking for us to meet you?" Like a mother about to scold her child, she was already at the top level of anger. "A text message?"

Thorn kept the same expression, doing his best not to add fuel to the fire.

Thorn's father continued to stare.

"Well," Liv hissed. "What the hell is going on? One moment, you two are happy. And then the next...I don't even know what happened. Thorn, straighten this out now." She turned to me, her eyes furious but not full of hate. "You better not have hurt my son, Titan. I don't care how much you mean to us. This is my baby and—"

"Mom." Thorn held up his hand, silencing her. "Let me talk, alright?"

I took the insult well because I'd been expecting a lot worse.

Liv was quiet, but she was practically shaking.

Thorn continued. "There's something I have to tell you guys. It's gonna be a lot to take in, and let me apologize beforehand. I lied to you...and I know I shouldn't have. It was the wrong thing to do."

"Lied about what?" Liv asked.

Thorn glanced at me before he kept going. "Titan and I have never been in love. While we love each other a great deal and we're very good friends, our romance was fabricated. I wanted a wife to have children, and she wanted a husband she could trust. We both wanted to have our physical relationships outside the marriage—"

"Are you gay?" Liv blurted.

Thorn was much more patient with her than he ever was with anyone else. "No. Neither is Titan."

"Oh…" Liv's eyebrows furrowed in confusion. "If neither one of you is gay, then what do you need a fake marriage for?"

"Well…" Thorn paused as he tried to figure out how to word it.

"I gave up on love." I wanted to give Thorn some time to come up with a suitable answer, so I took the lead. "I had a bad relationship when I was younger, and I didn't believe in men anymore. I wanted a husband who would love me unconditionally, who would never hurt me, and would be a great business partner. Thorn and I are very close, and I knew he would be a great father. Since he's my best friend, I thought he would be the perfect man to spend my life with."

Liv's mouth shut and her eyes narrowed. She didn't seem confused anymore, simply surprised. Thorn's dad still listened to the discussion, absorbing everything like a sponge.

Thorn added to the conversation. "I...I'm not really the kind of man who wants to settle down with a woman. I'm more... I like to be free." There was no easy way for a son to say this to his mother, that he preferred one-night stands with various flings. That he didn't do romance or commitment. He just wanted to fuck—simple as that. "But I do want a family, so I thought Titan and I could start one. We could be great partners and great friends. But I would retain my freedom to still enjoy the things I like."

Liv covered her mouth, clearly unsure what to say.

His father was speechless too.

"I'm sorry I lied," Thorn continued. "I lied to the whole world, and I lied to you. The reason it came apart was because Titan fell in love with someone else. We were already engaged and it was a complicated situation, but she decided she couldn't live without him. So don't get angry with

Titan. She did nothing wrong. I've seen other women, and she's seen other men. There was no cheating. Titan and I got into an argument about it and didn't speak for a while, but we're still as good of friends as we were before. We may not be getting married, but she'll always be a huge part of my life."

Liv finally looked at her husband, a silent conversation passing between them.

I didn't know what they would say in response. It was a delicate situation, an extremely awkward one.

More time passed. More silence.

I looked at Thorn, and he looked at me.

Finally, Liv Spoke. "Thorn...I don't know what to say." The disappointment was written all over her face. She didn't need to say it. "This is a shock to your father and me. This entire time we thought you loved Titan—"

"I do love her," Thorn said. "Just not romantically."

"Even so," Liv said. "I don't know why you felt the need to lie about it. You could have told us the truth, Thorn."

"I didn't think you would understand," Thorn said quietly. "It was easier to let the world believe we were in love."

"Thorn, if you want a family, why don't you fall in love and start one?" his mother asked.

Thorn clenched his jaw as he considered what to say. "I...I'm not interested in love. I know that's hard to understand, but I'm incapable of it."

"You are not incapable of it," she countered. "You're a wonderful man, Thorn. We couldn't be prouder of you. You have a heart that's so big and beautiful."

"You just haven't found the right one," his father said. "But when you do, you'll know."

Thorn didn't argue again, knowing they would never understand the way he felt. "Anyway...that's the truth. I'd like you to keep it to yourselves. It'll be a lot easier for us this way. And you have no reason to be angry with Titan. She's still my closest friend. She's still family to me."

"Of course," his mother said gently. "We'll always love Titan even if she's not your wife." Liv looked at me, the motherly affection back in her expression. "So...Diesel Hunt, huh?"

It was nearly impossible for me not to smile when his name was mentioned. "Yes."

"That is one good-looking man," Liv said with a laugh.

Thorn's father shot her a glare. "Is he now?"

"I'm just saying..." Liv brushed it off. "And his father...they don't make them like that anymore."

Thorn cringed. "Mom."

"Hey, it's something to think about," Liv said. "At least you'll know Diesel will still be a good-looking man when he gets older."

I had no doubt he would be a beautiful man for a very long time. His touch would always send shivers down my spine, and I would always need him. When we were old and gray, that attraction might dwindle, but we would love each other on a much deeper level. "I'm sure he will be."

"Do you like him, Thorn?" Liv asked. "He seems like the strong and silent type, but that's not a bad thing."

Thorn nodded. "I do like him. He's a good guy." It didn't seem like he was just giving the answer I wanted him to. It seemed like he meant it.

"We would love to meet him, Titan," Liv said. "Make sure he's good enough for you."

I'd always been jealous of Thorn for having both of his parents in his life. Having the unconditional love of a guardian was something you couldn't put a price on. But when they showered me with the same parental love, I felt like I was part of their family. "You guys will love him."

11

HUNT

I SLID into the booth across from Brett, still in my suit because I'd come immediately after work. He was in slacks and a gray collared shirt, his dark hair styled like he'd been somewhere important that afternoon. "Hey."

There was a noticeable tension in the air between us because we were both thinking about the exact same thing. "Hey." He was on his second beer, his first bottle off to the side and ready to be taken by the waiter.

I waved down the bartender and ordered what he was having. The second the cap was off, I took a deep drink. Right now, I had nothing but good things going on in my life. My relationship with my father wasn't perfect, but my woman was happy now that Thorn was back in the picture.

And that made me happy.

"Vincent said the same thing to me that he said to you." It was pointless to beat around the bush when the topic was so profound for both of us. Our father was trying to get back into our lives. He'd done terrible things to me, but what Brett had experienced was much worse. He was young at the time, much more vulnerable than he was now. Time had scarred him, and he'd turned into a man just like me. But he smiled more often—something I'll never understand.

"And what do you think about it?" He drank his beer again, taking bigger gulps than he usually would.

"I'm not sure. Seemed like he meant it."

"Yeah, I got the same impression." He rested his arms on the table, his shoulders slouched and the joy in his eyes gone. "I never would have agreed to meet him in a million years, and when I sat across from him, he said everything I didn't expect him to say. I thought I would hear excuses...but I didn't hear any of that."

"No."

"But I'm closer to forty than I am thirty, and I don't need him. When I was young, it was a different story. But so much time has passed, it seems like it's too late. What kind of relationship can we have now? What would be the point of it?"

"I see what you mean."

He sighed as he stared at his beer. "But I don't want to deny forgiveness to someone who's being sincere either. I've never been the kind of guy to hold a grudge. I let things go, and I'll live longer for it. But with Vincent...it's different. He told me I was never the problem, but he was jealous of my father. Couldn't handle it."

"He said the same to me."

"And he's not even my father...so we really don't need a relationship."

It was already difficult enough to connect with someone you were related to, but to share a connection with someone who was practically a stranger was even more difficult, especially when that person did terrible things.

"Whatever happens between us, I don't want it to influence your relationship with him." Brett picked at the label on the bottle, peeling the sticker away. "He is your flesh and blood, and he never did anything to you."

"You're my flesh and blood too, Brett. And he did do something to you."

His brown eyes narrowed in intensity. "You've

always been loyal to me, and I appreciate that. But he's apologized for his wrongdoing, so you have no reason to shut him out anymore. He made things right with me. Now you need to make things right with him."

It wasn't so easy; the situation wasn't black and white. "He did a lot of fucked-up shit to me."

"I know."

"I don't think I can sweep that under the rug."

"Don't blame you."

"But he seems sincere in his remorse. He's helped Titan with a lot of things. He's been good to both of us, kind and understanding. It's hard to say no to him when it seems like he's changed."

"If you want to forgive him, you should."

"I don't know…"

"You don't have to make a decision now. But don't let my feelings affect your decision."

"You think I should forgive him?" I asked.

He shrugged. "I can't answer that."

"I want your opinion, Brett."

He sighed before he took another drink of his beer. "If he's changed and he's living up to his word…maybe you should. At the end of the day, he is your father. He's in great shape, but he's not going to be around forever. If there's a possibility you can make things right and start over, why shouldn't you?"

"You really believe that?" I whispered.

He nodded. "Family is family."

"And you're my family, Brett."

"I know, man. I never met my father. Have no idea what he was like. The way I see it...you do have a father."

"He should have been a father to you too."

"It doesn't matter what he should have been...it's in the past. Honestly, I wished he loved me the way he loves the two of you. That always hurt the most... never being good enough."

I'd never heard Brett say anything like this. He was usually carefree and lighthearted. He didn't pour out his feelings like this. "It sounds like you can't forgive him."

"Sometimes I think I can. Sometimes I think I can't." He stared at the peeled wrapper on the table, the hard lines around his jaw more pronounced because of the tension. "What does Titan think?"

"That he deserves another chance."

"She's usually right about everything..."

"Yeah, but don't ever tell her that," I said with a chuckle.

He smiled back. "So, you guys are official now?"

"I'm sure you saw the headlines."

"She must be head over heels for you to go through all of that..."

"She is." I grinned like an idiot, remembering how she'd crawled into my bed the other night. A single night apart was too much for her. I didn't like it either, but it was nice to see her cave first.

"You're a lucky guy. Titan is a great woman. You couldn't have settled down with anyone better."

"Thanks, man."

"If she pities Vincent and even has a relationship with him...you may not have much of a choice. She's going to get her way on this."

Very true. Titan managed to manipulate me like she did the rest of the world—because I let her. "You're right. But she's going to do the same to you."

He scoffed. "Damn, you're right."

"Looks like we're both going down."

I clinked my beer against his. "You got that right."

I HAD JUST FINISHED ALL MY MEETINGS FOR THE afternoon when I wondered what I should do for lunch. Now I had the luxury to ask Titan to lunch whenever I felt like it. I could show up at her office without even needing a reason.

It was nice.

But my plans changed when Natalie spoke through the intercom. "Sir, Mr. Vincent Hunt is here to see you."

His random visits no longer caught me by surprise. An unexpected appearance could happen at any moment in time. Instead of just calling, he chose to speak to me in person. I wasn't sure if that was a gesture of respect on his part. "Send him in."

My father walked in a moment later, looking sleek in his three-piece suit. He was dressed in black, the dark color suiting his expression perfectly. Black was my preferred color as well. It fit our brooding demeanors.

When he reached my desk, he didn't take a seat. With one hand in his pocket, he stopped just a few feet away and stared at me with his typical look of confidence. He could be caught off guard, but his attitude would never change. All through my child-hood, he had always been that way. Always strong, quiet, and resilient. "I'm heading to lunch. Join me."

This would be the second time we would have lunch together, and it was beginning to become a routine. I wasn't sure if that was the kind of relationship I wanted, one where expectations would start. I sat in my chair as I stared at him, debating my decision.

"You can always say no, Diesel. I never want you to feel obligated."

I didn't feel obligated. A part of me actually wanted to go, and that scared me.

My father patiently waited for a more concrete answer.

"Alright."

He didn't question my decision. "What are you in the mood for?"

"Something light."

"I know just the place."

We left the office and walked a few blocks until we found a small deli. It wasn't a formal restaurant like it had been the first time, and the casual atmosphere made the situation less tense. We ordered our food separately then sat down.

He sat across from me at the table, eating a vegetarian sandwich with no pickles. He'd always hated pickles.

Without Titan there, it wasn't always easy to have a conversation. She somehow defused tense situations as a moderator. It kept everyone comfortable. A lifetime of working in challenging situations had given her an incredible wealth of knowledge and intuition. "I saw Brett yesterday."

My father opened a bag of chips and munched on a few. "How is he?"

"He's okay. Unsure how he feels about you."

"I don't blame him for being hesitant. He doesn't owe me anything."

My father was different from how he used to be, now extremely blunt about his shortcomings. He didn't show the stubbornness I was used to seeing. Transparent like glass, he made his thoughts easy to see. "What do you want from him?"

"Forgiveness. I thought I made that clear."

"Ideally," I said. "But what would you like from him?"

"Ideally..." He mulled over the word as he took a bite of his sandwich. He chewed slowly, taking his time before he finally swallowed. "If I could get my way, I would like to be on speaking terms with him. I'd like to be his friend. I'd like the opportunity to be family to him. Be something like a father to him... even though I know that would never happen."

"Because you want that? Or because Mom would want that?"

He pulled a chip out of the bag as he contemplated it. "Both. I'd always considered myself to be a father to two sons. I should have been a father to three. When I see your mother's eyes in his face, I should see him as mine. I know it's late, but I feel that way now. Perhaps he'll have the compassion to give me a chance to prove that to him...or maybe he won't."

When my father said things like that, I forgot about the terrible things he'd done. I forgot about the way he'd threatened me in my own office. All of that didn't seem to matter anymore when he sounded so sincere. I didn't see him as Vincent Hunt, but as a man who truly wanted a second chance.

I saw him as my father.

He placed another chip in his mouth and slowly chewed. "Thank you for having lunch with me. Even if we don't talk much, I enjoy looking up and seeing your face. I enjoy seeing you look back at me."

I hadn't taken a bite of my food in the entire interaction because I'd been too focused on him. His words were too raw for me to handle, so I continued to sit there in silence. When it came to Titan, I could say a lot of emotional things and not think twice about it, but outside our relationship, I couldn't digest and process emotions so easily.

My father didn't seem affected by my silence. "Titan and Thorn are getting along?"

Titan was a subject I could discuss all day. "Yeah. She's really happy."

"I'm glad he's had a change of heart."

"Me too." I didn't know what made Thorn change his mind, but I was glad he came to his senses. "I know she needs him to be happy, so I don't mind sharing her—at least, a little."

"Good friends are hard to find. We all need a few."

"Yeah..." I finally grabbed my sandwich and took a bite. "So, Alessia seems nice." We always talked about my love life. Maybe we should talk about his.

"I enjoy her company," he said bluntly. "But that's all." He didn't break his stride as he continued to eat, the subject of the conversation having no effect on his appetite.

"You ever think about getting remarried?" It was a question I'd never asked before because I'd never been in the position to. I saw him with a different woman every few months. Nothing ever seemed serious.

"No." His response was short, but he didn't seem annoyed by the question. His body language didn't change, and his appetite didn't wane.

"May I ask why?"

His tone remained the same. "Don't see the

point. I've already had my great love. I had her for a short time, made a family with her, and now she's gone. I already have my children, so I don't need a wife for that. I'll never fall in love again. Marriage doesn't benefit me in any way. I enjoy spending time with women like Alessia because they're young and beautiful. I lavish them with expensive gifts and trips around the world. We have a good time together. But once that fun starts to fade away, that's it. They need to find a husband, and I make it abundantly clear I'm not that man. Some of them think they'll change my mind if they spend enough time with me. But they never do."

If I lost Titan, I'd probably have the exact same outlook on life. She was the only woman I would ever love my entire life. There would never be someone after her. If she ever left or passed away, I'd fall into the same type of relationships. It was what I did before her. It was what I would do after her. "I used to feel that way until I met Titan. I thought I would be alone my entire life until I met her."

"Same thing happened to me. I met your mother, and just like that, my life completely changed. I knew I wanted to give her my entire life. So I did."

I wanted to give Titan everything I had.

"There's something I want to give you." He set his sandwich down and dug into his pocket.

I hadn't gotten a gift from him since my sixteenth birthday. Now I was a billionaire, so there was no monetary gift he could give me that would make an impact. Besides, money was the last thing I needed from him.

He pulled out a small black box and placed it on the table in front of me. There was no introduction or explanation. He watched me as he waited for me to open it.

"What is it?" I didn't touch it.

"Open it and you'll see."

I didn't like surprises, so I took my time opening it. I grabbed the sleek box and popped the lid open.

Inside was a white gold band with a solitary diamond in the center. The diamond wasn't monstrous like the one Thorn had given Titan. It was subtle, but the quality of the diamond was unprecedented. I took the ring out of the box and stared at it harder, realizing I'd seen it before. I focused on the inside of the band and saw the engraving in the metal. It was the date of my parents' wedding anniversary. When I understood exactly what I was holding, I shot my eyes back to my father.

His expression didn't change despite the gift he'd

just given me. "I'd always planned on giving that to whichever son got married first. Since it's you, I'm giving it to you. This isn't some attempt to earn your forgiveness. It's completely genuine."

I held my mother's ring in my hand, feeling the weight of my past. She'd been wearing it the day she had me. She wore it for decades. She wore it every single day until it was removed from her cold hands. "I can't take this…"

"Your mother would want you to have it."

"I'm not getting married right now."

He cocked an eyebrow. "Why not?"

Titan and I had just started dating each other seriously. I wanted to spend my life with her, but according to the media, it would seem too fast. Titan had already smeared her clean reputation telling the world about me. I couldn't expect her to marry me so quickly. "It's too soon."

His features hardened, as if I gave the wrong answer. "When you find the woman you can't live without, it's never too soon. Time will pass quickly, and when she's gone, that's the moment when you'll say it's too soon. Don't waste any time, Diesel. The clock is always ticking, and you have far less time than you think."

I felt the band in my fingertips, feeling my mother's love even though she wasn't on this earth anymore. My father bought her a ring that wasn't flashy or overly expensive. It wouldn't have suited her personality if it had been. It wouldn't have suited Titan's personality either. She was the richest woman in the world—she didn't need a man to buy her diamonds. "I'm not even sure if she would say yes."

"Diesel, that woman betrayed her best friend just to be with you. She's taken a second chance on love for you. She's taken your word over evidence. She told the entire world that you're her soul mate. Trust me, that woman will say yes—a million times. All you have to do is ask."

———

AFTER HITTING THE GYM, I HEADED TO TITAN'S penthouse.

It was empty. She was nowhere in sight, and judging by the fact that her purse wasn't hanging on the coatrack, she hadn't come home yet. I helped myself to the shower in the meantime, assuming she would be home any minute.

When I was finished, she still hadn't returned. I decided to call her.

She answered after a few rings. "Diesel." She said my name in the sexiest way, like she was teasing me on purpose.

"Baby. Where are you?"

"I'm out with Thorn. We're getting a drink at the bar."

I was happy she had Thorn back, and I could hear her joy pour out of the phone. It was a kind of happiness I'd never heard from her. I knew it wasn't just because of him, but because she had both of us in her life. "I just got out of the shower. Why didn't you tell me?"

"Tell you what?"

"That you were going out."

She immediately hardened. "I didn't realize I had to report to you, Diesel. I can't remember a time when I expected that from you."

I wasn't trying to take away her independence, and I should have known she would react that way if I tried. "That's not how I meant it. You know that. Just wanted to know why you weren't home."

"Thorn and I are drinking. You want to come?"

I wasn't jealous of Thorn, but I was jealous he was hogging all of her time lately. They seemed to be inseparable, going to lunch together or getting drinks after work. It would be selfish for me to intervene in that, but I missed having her all to myself. "It's alright. I'll see you when you get back."

"Come on," she said. "Get that hunky ass down here."

I grinned at her choice of words. "Hunky, huh?"

"Give me the phone." Thorn's voice was in the distance. It got louder when he took the phone away. "Hey, it's Thorn. Stop being a little bitch and get down here."

"Little bitch, huh?"

"Yeah," Thorn said. "I get you guys are an old boring couple now, but live a little. We're at the Hotspot. Hustle." Click.

I grabbed my jacket and left.

I SLID INTO THE BOOTH BESIDE TITAN, MY ARM naturally moving around her shoulders as I leaned in to kiss her.

She kissed me back, longer than usual for a public space. "What took you so long?" Her hand reached for my thigh, and she squeezed it just the way she grabbed me when we were in bed together.

I couldn't keep the smile off my face. "I got here in ten minutes."

"Still too long."

I brushed my lips along her hairline and pressed a kiss to her temple. "I'll make it up to you later."

"You better."

I turned to Thorn across the table, who was drinking his beer without caring about our affection. "How's it going, man?"

"Pretty good. The beer is just right, and we ordered a basket of cheese fries."

"You?" I cocked an eyebrow. "And you?" I turned back to Titan. She was the pickiest eater I knew, choosing to ignore food in favor of booze. She turned down any extra calories she didn't need just to maintain her figure. Still wasn't sure how she did it.

"We're living wild tonight," she said with a chuckle. "Want to join us?"

"If you guys are gonna eat poison, then I'll eat some poison too."

"Good," Thorn said. "You're a team player. I respect that."

My arm slid down to her waist, and I kept my hand on her opposite hip because I loved touching her. I was out in public with Titan on my arm, her old fiancé sitting across from us. We were enjoying life, not caring what anyone thought of us. It was a nice feeling, long overdue. "How are things with your parents?"

"Better," Thorn said as he kept his hand on his glass. "Titan and I talked it over, and they were still pretty confused about the whole thing. It's difficult to explain to your mother that you're a manwhore and you're always going to be a manwhore. I told her I was incapable of love, and that was something she couldn't grasp. But that's how mothers are...always see the best in you even when it's not there." He lifted the glass to his lips and downed his scotch.

"Well, that's inaccurate." I motioned to the bartender to give me the same drink Titan was having.

"Inaccurate?" Thorn challenged. "Trust me, it's not."

"You love Titan, don't you?"

"Obviously," Thorn said coldly. "But not in the way you love her. I've known her for over ten years, have been through hell with this woman, and out of all that life experience, I never fell in love with her. You don't find that strange?" He rattled the ice cubes in his glass. "She's the perfect woman. She's ambitious, beautiful, funny...what more could a guy ask for? But you know what?" He shook his head. "I've never felt anything. Nothing. And if I haven't felt anything for this woman, no other woman on this planet stands a chance."

I was relieved he wasn't in love with my woman. But I also thought things would have been different if the circumstances were changed. "If you were sleeping together, I think your feelings would have changed."

Thorn shook his head. "I doubt that too." He turned to Titan. "No offense."

"None taken," she said with a chuckle.

"And I'm not here to argue about it," Thorn said. "But my decision is set in stone. Love isn't for me. Never has been. Never will be. Maybe I can find another woman who would be interested in having the same arrangement, but I highly doubt it. It worked for Titan and me because we had the exact same needs. But what are the chances of that happening again?" He shook his drink and took a quick sip. "None."

Titan massaged my muscular thigh under the table, her fingertips pressing through my jeans. "His parents don't hate me, so that's nice. But they were definitely disappointed when they heard the truth. I think telling them was the right thing to do because they seemed more upset by that than the actual facts."

"Yeah," Thorn said in agreement. "And now I don't have to lie anymore. That's nice." He shifted his gaze back to me. "So you and Vincent are working things out?"

I should have assumed Titan would have told him everything by now. "We're on speaking terms, but that's about it."

"He doesn't seem like the kind of guy that takes no for an answer." Thorn was still in his suit from earlier that afternoon, a gray one with a pink tie. "When he told me about your relationship, it seemed like he was never going to give up."

My eyes narrowed as I processed what he said. At what occasion had Vincent and Thorn spoken to each other? Was it the gala last weekend? "When did this conversation happen?"

"Last week," Thorn said. "He came by my office."

My eyes narrowed further, my anger rising. My father already went to extremes to repair his relationship with me, but to go to Thorn was simply excessive. "To discuss my family drama?"

Titan released her grip on my thigh, her touch becoming soothing. "No. He actually talked to Thorn about forgiving me. Said he regretted the last ten years and didn't want Thorn to go through the same thing."

"He seemed sincere," Thorn said. "Told me it would be stupid to let Titan go. Time would pass, and I would only find myself feeling miserable rather than vindicated. He made me realize it would be worse to look back in regret than to forgive. So that's what I did." His eyes shifted back to Titan. "And I'm glad I did."

My expression didn't change because my thoughts were still focused on the revelation he'd just made. My father never mentioned this to me, not even when I saw him the other day. He intervened in Titan's relationship and did what he could to make Thorn forgive her. I'd never asked him to do that, and he didn't seem to want any credit for it. Having Thorn back in Titan's life meant more to me than I could put into words. Gratitude flooded from every organ, and I nearly forgot to breathe.

Titan studied my expression, knowing something was wrong. "Everything okay, Diesel?"

I swallowed and felt the dryness of my throat. "Yeah...I didn't realize my father did that."

"I meant to tell you," Titan said. "We've been so busy that it kept slipping my mind."

My hand slid from her waist as the bartender placed my glass in front of me. Immediately, I wrapped my fingers around it and took a drink. The amber liquid moistened my throat and brought a burn to my stomach. My father used to be my greatest enemy. He wanted to destroy me like he did everyone else who got in his way. But underneath all that hatred was a father aching for his son. I couldn't see it at the time because I didn't believe anything good could be covered in something so spiteful. But perhaps my father really meant every word he said. Maybe he really had changed. Maybe he was in far more pain than I realized.

Titan moved her hand up my arm, gently touching me. "Diesel?"

I'd forgotten Titan and Thorn were there altogether. Memories of my childhood flashed across my mind. I remembered the horrible things he did to Brett, and I could actually understand his actions. My sympathy had changed my perception, even though his actions were still unforgivable. "I'm fine." I downed the rest of my glass in a single gulp and slid out of the booth. "I just remembered I have to be somewhere." I ignored the concerned expression on Titan's face and didn't look at Thorn at all. I stepped out of the restaurant and immediately got into the first cab I saw because I didn't want Titan to follow me.

She couldn't help me with this.

No one could.

———————

I LEFT ONE BAR AND WOUND UP IN ANOTHER.

It was a sports bar right next to my penthouse. The game was shown on every single TV, and groups of friends dined on finger food and beer while they cheered and booed every time the score changed. I was surrounded by social cacophony, but the distraction was welcomed.

I didn't want to think about my father.

It was nice not to think about anything.

My phone lit up with a text message. *I understand if you want to be alone right now, but just tell me you're alright.*

I could hear the concern in her voice even though she didn't speak. She'd been nothing but good to me, and I wasn't going to risk losing her by pushing her away. The only thing I should be doing right now was pulling her closer. *I'm watching the game at a bar across the street from my place.*

Thank you. I'll talk to you later. Like she said she would, she left me alone.

I wanted to be alone—but I wanted to be alone with her. *Where are you?*

Home.

I'll be right there.

Diesel, I understand if you need your space.

I've gotten enough space.

I left the cash on the counter and took a cab to her place a few blocks over. I rode the elevator to the top floor then stepped into her living room. She was sitting on the couch dressed in just my t-shirt and her panties. Instead of having another helping of liquor, she had a glass of water on the coffee table.

Without anger or sadness, she looked me over with a soft expression. All she seemed to care about was me, not the way I'd stormed out of the bar a few hours ago. She pulled her knees to her chest and left her laptop on the coffee table. "Hey."

"Hey." I fell into the cushion beside her and rested my hand between her thighs. She didn't exercise regularly anymore, but she still had incredible legs. My fingertips gently massaged her soft skin, feeling the warmth of both of our bodies combined together.

Her makeup had been washed away, so she'd obviously expected me to stay away for the rest of the night. When her foundation was gone, her gorgeous complexion was on display. With a tiny freckle in the corner of her mouth and one right in the center of her right cheek, she was the kind of natural beauty that didn't exist often. When the mascara and eyeliner were gone, her eyes didn't stand out as much, but they showcased a deep layer of her soul.

"I'm sorry I stormed out like that."

"It's really okay, Diesel." Her voice as soft as a feather, it floated over my skin and gently caressed me. "We all handle information differently. Nothing to be sorry about."

"When Thorn said that about my father...I wasn't sure how to process it. It seems like he always puts our best interest first. I had lunch with him the other day, and he never mentioned his conversation with Thorn...as if he didn't want the recognition."

"I think he just wanted to protect Thorn's privacy."

"You're probably right. But even then...he did that for you. He knew it would make you happy, which would make me happy. Slowly, he's tugging away at my armor and ripping it off piece by piece. Now I'm gradually forgetting all the terrible things he did and focusing on the good... I can't control it."

She hooked her arm through mine and placed a kiss on my shoulder. "You want to forgive him."

"I don't know," I whispered. "For the past ten

years, I've hated him. And now that he's said the right things and done the right things...I don't hate him anymore."

"But do you really want to keep hating him?" she whispered.

I stared at the floor. "I don't know...I just think it's happened so quickly."

"But it hasn't. It's been months, Diesel. And when it comes to family, you should never hate each other. Vincent did terrible things, but he apologized for them. He's different now. There's nothing more he can do. Not once did he ever make excuses for what he did. He owned up to them, apologized, and then moved on. That's all you can ask for from anyone."

I continued to stare at the floor, thinking about the last conversation I'd had with my father. "Brett isn't sure if he can forgive him, but he doesn't want that to affect my relationship with him."

"It shouldn't," she said in agreement. "Brett is a completely different situation."

"I still feel like I'm betraying him."

"You aren't, Diesel. This is your father. You know your mother would want you to be together, not apart."

Now that my mother's ring was sitting in my

nightstand, I felt connected to her in a way I hadn't since she died. It reminded me how much my father loved my mother, how their love was eternal, even now. He'd made a lot of mistakes, but when a man was swallowed up by that kind of grief, there was no telling what he might do. He held a vigil for her in his heart, unable to find love again because it was impossible for him to love another woman besides the one he married. My sympathy had changed my opinion of him, leading to a calm sense of under-standing.

Titan rubbed her hand up and down the center of my back. "You want to know what I think?"

I knew she was really asking, offering her advice only if I wanted to hear it. I gave a slight nod.

"I think Vincent is ashamed of who he used to be. I think he's a different man than you used to know. I think he loves you, and I think he even loves Brett too. If you decided to cut him out of your life for good, you wouldn't be doing yourself a favor. You wouldn't be protecting yourself from anyone. And Vincent will have to suffer the rest of his life knowing he has a son he'll never get to be with. You're dooming each of you to a bitter and painful existence."

Titan was the smartest person I knew, and any

advice she ever gave was solid. She could remove the emotional part of the situation and stare at it objectively. She could see past the details to the foundation of any given situation. Despite the hard life she'd lived and the ruthless people who'd tried to hurt her, she rose above it and still saw the good in other people. She saw the goodness in my father—because there was something to see.

"But you have to make this decision on your own, Diesel. I can't make it for you. I'll stand by whatever choice you make."

"It's hard for me to believe we could have a new relationship. So much time has passed, so much heartbreak. But then I look at us now...and we already do have a relationship. It's tense and uncomfortable, but it's there. I asked him about Alessia, and he was open with me. He asked me about you...I was open with him. There's a dialogue...a conversation. There's something there."

She ran her fingers through my hair. "And it's worth fighting for."

BRETT AND I MET FOR LUNCH AT A TABLE WITH THREE menus.

He sat down and noticed the third place setting. "Titan coming?"

I ambushed him, using the same technique Titan was known for. "No."

Brett's eyebrows slowly rose toward his forehead. "This can't be good..."

"I invited my father."

"Because...?"

"I think we should all sit down and talk."

"Diesel, I told you I didn't care what you decided to do. But you should respect my wishes as well."

"And I do," I said calmly. "But the three of us haven't been in the same room together in a decade. I think we should see where it goes."

"You know, I expected this from Titan—but not you." He crossed his arms over his chest, wearing a black leather jacket with a dark blue V neck underneath.

"I learned from the best." I tried to keep it light-hearted despite how dramatic the situation was. "He doesn't know you're going to be here either. So you're both equally unprepared."

His eyes shifted to the right when he spotted something. "Here he is."

My father walked toward the table, not affected by Brett's unexpected presence at all. As if he'd been expecting him the entire time, he greeted us both with a look before he took a seat. He didn't shake our hands or make any other kind of gesture.

He sat perfectly upright then took a drink from his water glass.

Like any other time I was with my father, it was tense.

Extremely tense.

My father turned his gaze on Brett, paying more attention to him than he did to me. "It's nice to see you, Brett."

All Brett gave was a nod.

I'd brought all three of us together, but I wasn't sure what to do now. "The three of us haven't had a conversation together in...a really long time. I thought we could talk, maybe clear the air."

Brett stared at his menu.

My father kept looking at him.

I stared at both of them. Maybe this was a bad idea.

"I recently bought one of your cars, the new edition of the Bullet." My father removed his phone from his pocket and pulled up a picture. It was dark gray and sleek, a brand-new version of the car I'd bought just a few months ago. "It's smooth. Before I realize what I'm doing, I've hit ninety before I'm even off the ramp and onto the highway." He set the phone next to Brett so it was easily visible.

Brett shifted his gaze to the screen and stared it for several minutes, probably noticing slight details no one else picked up on. "She's beautiful."

"Thank you."

Brett returned the phone.

My father slid it back into his pocket. "I bought her last week. She's sitting in my garage along with the rest of my collection, but I think she might be my favorite. For a luxury car, she has something special the others lack. It's not just the engine, but the whole experience. The sound system is the highest quality I've ever seen—and that's saying something because I own a lot of cars." It didn't seem like he was sucking up to Brett, just talking about something they had in common.

Brett didn't remain stubborn for long. "Thank you. I take great pride in my work."

"It shows." Vincent picked up the menu and scanned it despite the heaviness in the room. "Are you working on anything else?"

"I'm taking a break, actually," Brett said. "I spent a long time designing that model. Need some time to come up with new ideas."

"Understandable." My father looked at me. "What are you getting, Diesel?"

I hadn't even looked at the menu yet. I picked something at random. "The Cobb."

My father looked relaxed in his chair, taking control of an awkward conversation with a noticeable level of class. It wasn't surprising that he was so persuasive when he could handle difficult conversations like this. "I think I'll get the same. What about you, Brett?"

"I'm not a salad kinda guy. I'm getting a steak."

My father wore a slight smile. "Excellent choice." He set his menu down just when the waiter came over. We all ordered our drinks and food, and we were alone once more shortly afterward. My father rested his elbows on the armrests and brought his fingertips together, still looking casual. "How's business?"

"It usually picks up around this time of year," Brett said. "You know, the holidays."

My father nodded in understanding.

"Come January, it'll be slow," Brett said. "That's when I usually go on vacation."

"Where are you traveling to?" Vincent asked.

"Hawaii," Brett answered. "Where they don't have blizzards."

My father nodded in agreement. "Taking anyone along?"

"Yeah." Brett didn't elaborate on the guest list. He didn't talk about his personal life much, not even to me. Women came and went, sexy flings that he enjoyed. He'd been looking for the right woman for a long time, but she'd never come along. Women like Titan didn't grow on trees. "What about you?"

"What about me?" my father asked.

"Taking any trips soon?" Brett asked.

"No," my father answered. "I usually spend the holidays alone. After the new year, I might jet off to somewhere with a warmer climate, but I haven't made plans this year. A woman I'm seeing asked me to spend the holidays with her and her family in Milan. I declined."

I never wondered what my father did over the holidays. I usually spent them with Brett. I guess my father spent them alone.

Brett was obviously surprised Vincent had told him something somewhat personal. His eyebrows were furrowed. "Not serious, then?"

"No," my father said quickly. "None of them is. I usually stop by the cemetery early in the morning. Christmas used to be special to your mother and me. We would each find each other a special ornament, and we would exchange it Christmas morning. So I bring her one every year." Despite how incredibly sad the story was, he didn't flinch. His voice remained perfectly steady, completely emotionless.

I'd gone to the cemetery on Christmas before. I'd noticed a glass ornament with an angel inside. I'd assumed one of my mother's friends had stopped by. It didn't seem like something my father would bring. Since I never saw him visit, I just assumed he never went. I guessed I was wrong.

I used to see my father as a large brute without a single feeling. Now I realized he was emotionally complicated, carrying a web of different heartaches and feelings. Just because he didn't wear his heart on his sleeve didn't mean he wasn't sensitive and loving. He remained rigid and strong like every man should be, but beneath that hard exterior, he was just a fragile as the rest of us.

Brett obviously hadn't been expecting that either, because he stared at him in complete silence.

After the silence stretched on for nearly a minute, Vincent broke it. "I think about you a lot, Brett. Probably doesn't seem like it, but I do. When I read headlines about you in the papers, it makes me happy to know you're doing so well. You're very well respected in the industry."

Brett stilled at the comment, processing it slowly. Then he finally nodded, clearing his throat at the same time. "Thanks..."

"Your mother would be proud of both of you," Vincent said confidently. "Not so much of me...but that's something I'll have to deal with later." He didn't wear his wedding ring even though he spoke like he was still married. I wondered if he said the same thing to his lovers. He was so rich and good-looking that they probably didn't care.

"Yeah," I added. "I think she would be too."

Now Brett looked at Vincent, no longer as guarded as before.

"I know you guys don't owe me anything, but it would mean a lot to me if the two of you met up with Jax. The three of you shouldn't have been separated to begin with. I know it would mean a lot to him as well."

"He wants to talk to us?" Brett asked.

"Of course he does," Vincent answered. "His only hesitance is me. He thinks you don't have a high opinion of him since he took my side..."

I'd never held it against Jax. I knew the situation was complicated.

"I don't feel that way," Brett said. "I'd like to see him."

"Yeah?" Vincent asked. "I'll let him know. Maybe the three of you could get a drink...catch up."

We spent the rest of the lunch making small talk about work and sports. The conversation never truly relaxed, but it wasn't unnerving either. My father managed to keep it smooth, using his special skills in language to keep the conversation flowing. No subject would ever be strong enough to detract from the reality of our situation.

Toward the end, Brett eyed his watch. "I've got to get going. I've got a meeting." He rose from his chair and pulled some cash from his wallet. He set it on the table in preparation for the bill that hadn't come yet. "I'll see you later, Diesel."

"Yeah, sure," I said, wondering if he would say anything to my father.

He looked at Vincent next, drawing a blank as to what to say next.

My father rose to his feet and extended his hand. "It's always a pleasure seeing you, Brett. I hope I see more of you."

I thought Brett wasn't going to take his hand because he didn't even raise his arm. He stared at my father's outstretched greeting as he considered it, not moving. Then he did the unexpected and placed his hand in his. "Yeah. Maybe."

They shook hands.

And then Brett walked out.

My father sat back down, looking forward with eyes filled with heavy thoughts.

I wasn't sure what I'd just witnessed, the beginning of a reconciliation or mere politeness.

My father drank his iced tea then checked his watch. He must not have anywhere important to be because he continued to sit there with his legs crossed and his elbows on the armrests. When the waiter brought the check, my father didn't immediately reach for it, and neither did I. We weren't doing the check dance, but paying the bill didn't seem urgent right now.

I expected he had something to say. I could feel it in the air between us. It was a sixth sense I had from growing up with a father like him. I picked up on his quiet moods, his slight shift in atmosphere.

"I know you did that for me, Diesel. You have no idea how much I appreciate it." He didn't look directly at me, which was unusual for him because he constantly maintained eye contact. But now he focused his gaze elsewhere. "I think there's hope for us. When I sit with him, I don't feel the sense of hatred I used to feel. Like his mother, he's far too compassionate to feel that way for long."

"I don't think he ever hated you," I said quietly. "I think he just wanted to be loved as much as Jax and I were. He said that's what hurt him the most."

My father closed his eyes briefly, swallowing the words like acid. They clearly affected him, making his straight physique seem slightly crooked. "Goddammit." He said the curse quietly, under his breath, so I could barely hear it.

"But you're right. I think he's coming around."

"And I know you wouldn't have done that unless you were coming around too." He turned his head and directed his gaze on me, staring at me with those customary dark eyes. His face was a mirror of my future, my appearance when time caught up to me. "Are you?"

I wanted to tell him I would never forgive him for what he did, but I couldn't. Right now, I pitied him. I saw a father who would do anything to have his son back. All his past crimes seemed irrelevant now that so much had changed. "I'm not saying everything is perfect between us...but I'm willing to forget the past and move forward. I'm willing to start over."

My father closed his eyes again, but this time, for much longer. His hand covered his face, and he slowly dragged it down, digesting my words like they were shards of glass. When he dropped his hand

and opened his eyes, a thin film of moisture coated the surface. A slightly red tint had already developed, and he wore a heavy expression he'd never worn before. My father was manly, cold, and rigid. The only appearance he ever broadcast was strength. But now, all the strength had been shed, and there was nothing but vulnerability. He was still a man, just a man stripped of wealth, strength, and power. What was left was just a man—a man who only cared about his son. "Thank you." He pivoted in his chair toward me, extending his hand.

I eyed it but didn't take it. I looked up at him again, seeing the desperation in his eyes. He kept his hand extended even though I chose to ignore it. I rose to my feet instead and opened both of my arms.

My father didn't move, shocked by the gesture. He lowered his hand and cleared his throat, the emotion increasing in his eyes. He rose to his feet, his eyes level with mine. He didn't blink the moisture away, almost proud of his impending tears. "Son..." He wrapped his arms around me and hugged me like a child, his powerful arms circling me with the strength of a bear.

I hugged him back, feeling his hard chest against mine. The last time I'd hugged my father was when I was in college, and even then, it was brief. We hadn't embraced like this since my mother died. He'd hugged me at her funeral, using my strength to keep himself upright. Maybe this was a mistake, but I refused to believe it was. It was so much better to let go of my anger and pain. It felt so much better to forget the past and embrace the future. It was a risk, but it was a risk I was willing to take. "Dad..."

JUST WHEN I finished setting the table, Diesel walked into the kitchen after his shower. His hair was still slightly damp, and he was just in his black sweatpants. When he wore them low on his hips, the V from his muscles was noticeable. His body was a work of art, so hard and rigid I wanted to drag my tongue along the grooves.

We took turns making dinner at night, and since I was home first, I threw something together. It was a vegan dish with tofu and vegetables. I tried to eat clean a few times a week, and Diesel never made a complaint because he was a picky eater too.

He had to be picky to look like that.

We sat together at the table and ate quietly. Diesel had his eyes trained on me most of the time, like watching me was his form of entertainment.

I found excessive eye contact to be hostile when it came to strangers, but with Diesel, it only made me feel owned. I was his personal property, and he could stare at me all he wanted. That didn't bother me one bit. "How was your day?"

He took another bite, chewing slowly and taking his time. When it was just the two of us in private, he ate with his arms on the table, shirtless with gorgeous tanned skin. He dropped his manners but retained his grace. "You want the bad news first? Or the good news?"

I wished there weren't bad news at all. "Bad."

"I have to go to California for a few days."

That was bad news. We hadn't been separated for so long since we found each other again. I didn't want to sleep in a different bed on the other side of the country. The sheets would be cold, and his smell would be gone. "How long?"

"I'm supposed to be there for five days, but I think I can cut it down to three."

"Can you cut it down even more?" My leg rubbed against his calf under the table.

"I would if I could, baby. Why don't you come along?"

I had way too much stuff to do in the city. "That's not an option."

He kept eating, his shoulders falling slightly. "Hopefully, the time goes by fast, then."

"Yeah..." Three days seemed like an eternity, but if I stayed busy, it shouldn't be too bad. "What's the good news?"

He finished chewing his food before he set down his fork altogether. Whatever he was about to say was significant. "I had lunch with Brett and my father today. We talked for a long time, and then Brett left. Basically...I forgave my father."

His relationship with his father didn't directly affect me, but it made me think of my own father. I missed him every day, and I wanted Diesel to know his father while there was still time. The last thing I wanted was for Diesel to live with regret. It was never too late to forgive, to start over. "I'm so happy to hear that."

"He tried to shake my hand, but I hugged him instead. It's been so long since I hugged my father..." His eyes trailed back down to his food. He didn't seem thrilled the way I was, but he didn't seem sad either. He was simply emotional.

"Do you feel better?"

"I wouldn't say I feel better," he said quietly. "I just...I think I made the right decision. I don't want to keep hating him. It seems like he's a different man now. Holding a grudge would only hurt me in the end."

I was glad he saw it that way. "And Brett?"

"I think he's coming around. Just needs more time."

"I'm sure your father is happy."

He gave a slight nod. "I've never seen my father cry before..."

Like someone punched me right in the heart, I felt my blood stop circulating just for an instant. Vincent Hunt was a strong man just like his son. To see someone like that succumb to such a raw emotion was surreal.

"He didn't cry. He just...got tears in his eyes. But that's the most I've ever seen from him."

"Even when your mother died?"

He shook his head. "He didn't cry in public...but I'm sure he did when he was alone."

"Yeah..."

Diesel was quiet for another minute before he picked up his fork again. He started to eat.

"What now?" I asked.

"With my father?"

"Yeah."

"I don't know. I guess we'll find out."

DIESEL PACKED HIS SUITCASE AND CARRIED IT TO THE door. He was taking his private plane to California, and he was leaving at the usual time we both went to work. He was in black jeans and a long-sleeved gray shirt, the fabric hugging the muscles of his body. His trip was short, but it still seemed like he was leaving for a lifetime.

I'd never been so dependent on another person for my happiness. I'd never been so clingy with a man, dreading sleeping in a bed alone. I used to demand my space, kicking a man out of my front door because I had no other use for him. But now I needed Diesel for everything.

He turned around and gave me a sad look, like he was as apprehensive about this short separation as I was. "It'll be over before you know it." His large arms circled my waist, and he looked down into my face with a cleanly shaven jaw.

"I know."

Diesel was going to California to oversee a real estate company he owned. They specialized in apartments and condos all across Southern California, along with beachfront property for the wealthy. He squeezed my waist with his fingertips, his dark eyes digging deep into mine.

"When will you be back?"

"Wednesday, around three in the morning. I'll see you after work."

That wasn't so far away. I could make it.

"I'll call you every night." He leaned in and kissed me.

I kissed him back, my hands moving to his strong shoulders. My fingertips dug into the fabric and into his muscles, remembering the way I'd grabbed him last night as he made love to me. He'd spent the evening buried inside me, as if we were going to be apart for weeks rather than days.

He pulled away then placed a kiss in the corner of my mouth. "Love you."

I never got tired of hearing that phrase, of staring at his lips as he mouthed the special words. Diesel Hunt was the love of my life, the man who had my soul in the palm of his hand. I loved him with everything I had, and I could see the way he loved me so fiercely. He was my perfect counterpart, just stronger and more rugged. "I love you too."

He kissed me on the forehead before he released me. "Have fun with Thorn."

"I'll try. But I'll probably miss you too much."

He grinned as he walked into the elevator with his bag. He turned around and hit the button. "You're obsessed with me."

I crossed my arms and fought the smile from stretching on my lips, knowing he was just teasing me. "Am not."

"Whatever you say, baby." The doors shut.

Once he was gone, I took a deep breath. I refused to be one of those women who came apart the instant their man was gone. There was a lot to do, and I shouldn't fixate on his absence. I had a lot more fulfillment in my life.

My phone lit up with a text message. *I'm more obsessed with you.*

"I HAVE VINCENT HUNT HERE FOR YOU," JESSICA SAID into the intercom.

Now when I heard that announcement, I didn't flinch in dread. "Send him in." Vincent had become an integrated part of my life. Just as Thorn could come by my office whenever he felt like it, Vincent could do the same thing.

He walked in a moment later, looking like a powerful executive with an impressive amount of control. He had the same stance as Diesel, the same silent authority that his son carried. They were more alike than either of them realized. He stopped at my desk and extended his hand. "Good afternoon, Titan. It's always nice to see you."

I eyed his hand but didn't take it. "I don't think we need to be so formal anymore."

He slowly lowered his hand and placed it in his pocket. "Diesel told you about our conversation."

"He did. I'm happy for you two."

He took a deep breath and let out a quiet sigh. "I haven't slept so well in forever...now I'm out like a light. It's like a huge weight has been lifted off my chest."

"I'm glad to hear that."

"I know things won't be perfect, but it means the world to me that I have my son back, that he's willing to move forward with me. I know you're responsible for that, and I can't thank you enough, Titan."

I only wanted the best for Diesel. His well-being would always come first. That was how a true relationship should be, when both partners gave everything to each other. Without concrete proof of Diesel's innocence, I decided to follow my heart and give him all of me—every single piece. "You don't need to thank me, Vincent."

"Well, I do anyway." He lowered himself into the chair facing my desk and crossed his legs.

I sat down as well, my arms resting on the surface of my desk. "Diesel said Brett still isn't quite there."

"No, he's not." His hands rested on the armrests, just the way Diesel's did when he sat in my office. "But he can take all the time he wants. I'm not his father so he doesn't owe me anything, but I hope we can reconcile. I would rather him be the fourth member of our family than live out there alone."

"He'll come around. He's a very sweet man. I've always liked Brett, even before I knew he was related to Diesel. He's respectful, thoughtful, and loyal. He treats me differently from other men, like a person rather than a woman."

"Well, his mother was wonderful."

"And you also set a good example for him."

Vincent looked away, as if my words insulted him instead of flattered him.

"Diesel has always been respectful toward me since the day we met. He's never been a sexist prick like the others. He admires my independence and isn't threatened by my success. Not once did he try to undermine me or patronize me. I'm constantly having to prove myself to my peers because men still think business and women don't mix. But Diesel is the kind of man that's so secure in his masculinity he's never been threatened by me. In fact, he admires my success. He loves my brains as well as my body. He's a fine man, and I'm proud to call him mine. He's obviously been influenced by someone—and I can tell that person is you." While Vincent had been my enemy in the past, he always treated me as an equal. He'd never talked down to me or looked at me in an inappropriate way.

Vincent turned back to me, his eyes soft as if my words meant something to him. "Every father wants to hear that...thank you. I'm very proud of my son. I should tell him that more often..."

"Now you have your chance, Vincent."

He gave a slight nod. "You're right. I do."

Silence stretched between us for nearly a minute, but it wasn't heavy with tension. It contained quiet reflection.

Vincent cleared his throat when he was ready to speak again. "Diesel is in California for a few days?"

"Yeah. He had business to take care of."

"I see. If you need anything while he's gone, you can always call me."

It was a sweet offer, so I didn't reject it right away. I was a strong woman who overcame everything that came my way. I didn't need the offer at all. "Thanks."

"I actually stopped by because I have a business opportunity for you."

Business was my entire world. "I'm listening."

"I'm putting my offer back on the table." Once we discussed business, we both immediately fell into our stride. It was the one thing we were both good at. "I can get your products in stores all over the world, not just China. I'm willing to offer you seventy percent of all sales."

It was a great deal, something I would snatch up instantly. But unfortunately, I couldn't do that. "That's a great offer, but I can't take it."

"I hope it's not because of our personal relationship," he said. "We both have the maturity to keep business separate."

"No, that's not why, Vincent. I've already established a partnership with Kyle Livingston."

Vincent stared at me sternly, like that information meant nothing to him. "You can end your arrangement with him since a better offer has been presented. It's just business. He'll understand that."

I operated under a different code of ethics. "He could have done business with you, but he chose to take a chance on me. I see Kyle as a partner, and I don't betray my partners. As much as I would like the opportunity, my reputation in business is more important to me." Vincent knew it was my biggest goal to hit every market in the world. It was a big project, and it wasn't easy to accomplish. Having a corporate veteran like him help me would be ideal. But I considered Kyle to be a friend at this point.

Vincent gave a slight nod. "I respect your decision."

"Thank you."

"So what if I extended the offer to both you and Kyle?"

I was taken aback by the surprise offer. "Both of us?"

"Same terms," he said. "You could still be partners, but you use me as a distributor. I get you where you want to be, and I take a thirty percent cut. It's a win-win for both of us."

It was a generous offer. He and Diesel had already made up, so I knew he wasn't trying to get something out of me. "You're sure?"

"Yes. Talk it over with Kyle and let me know."

"Just because I'm seeing Diesel doesn't mean you have to do me any favors, Vincent. Just want you to know that."

He gave me a slight smile. "I know, Titan."

AT MIDNIGHT, DIESEL CALLED ME.

"Baby." It was the first thing he said when I answered the phone.

"Hey." I was sitting on the couch with a glass of red wine. "How's it going over there?"

"The weather is nice. Almost too hot for jeans."

"It snowed today."

He chuckled. "I feel like I'm on the other side of the world, not the country."

"It feels that way to me too."

He was quiet for a while. "What are you doing?"

"Sitting on the couch."

"What are you wearing?"

I nearly rolled my eyes. "You know what I'm wearing."

"My shirt?" he asked.

"Yes. I'm wearing your boxers too."

"Ooh...that's sexy."

"That I'm dressed like a man?" I teased.

"That my woman misses me like crazy."

"I never said I missed you."

The arrogance was heavy in his voice. "But we both know you do."

"So what? You miss me."

"Fuck yeah, I miss you. I have this big bed but no woman to share it with."

I lay down on the couch with my feet over the armrest. I wished he were there with me now, sitting on the couch in just his sweatpants. I wished he could lay his heavy body on top of mine and smother me.

"How was your day?" he asked.

"Your father offered to be a distributor for Kyle and me."

"He did?" he asked in surprise. "Both of you?"

"He initially only made the offer to me, but I said I couldn't pull out of my deal with Kyle. It would be a betrayal if I did."

"You've always been loyal. I respect that."

Diesel never hesitated to flatter me, showing his respect every single day. Some men felt insecure, and as a result, he spat out an insult or two.

"Have you spoken to Kyle about it?"

"He's on board. So we're going to take the deal."

"That's great. If there's one thing you can trust with my father, it's he knows how to do business. I think you'll be in good hands."

"Me too."

We sat in silence for a while, enjoying the quiet company we shared. It was late and I should get to bed, but I suspected I wouldn't be getting much sleep tonight. It was strange not having him there with me.

After what seemed like five minutes, he spoke again. "I'm three hours behind, but I'm pretty tired. I'm going to get some sleep."

"Me too."

"I love you, baby."

"I love you too," I repeated back.

"Good night."

I almost didn't say it back. "Good night."

THORN INTERLOCKED HIS FINGERS BEHIND HIS HEAD and rested his crossed ankles on my desk. "Getting laid is more complicated now. After all this drama hit the media, women have a much different opinion of me. They either think I'm some heartbroken man looking for a rebound, or they think I'm the biggest player in the world."

I snapped my fingers and pointed to the ground, silently commanding him to get his feet off my desk. "You are the biggest player in the world."

"Yeah, but the entire world didn't use to think that."

"How did you explain our relationship to women before? They just thought you were cheating on me?"

"Open relationship," he explained. "But honestly, I don't think they cared. They just wanted me to give them good sex and buy them pretty things. People say men are shallow, but women are worse, if you ask me."

I narrowed my eyes.

"Some women," he corrected. "Not all."

I snapped my fingers again. "Get your feet off my desk."

He sighed before he lowered them to the ground. "It's comfy."

"I don't care how comfy it is."

"So, when's Diesel gonna be home?"

The mention of my lover immediately brought me down. I sighed before I answered. "Late tomorrow night."

"That's not too far away."

"For you..." My penthouse had never felt so empty. It was quiet and cold.

"Maybe you should get a cat or something."

"You know I don't have the time to take care of it."

"Cats don't need to be taken care of. Just get a litter box."

"You think I want my place to smell like cat shit?" I asked incredulously.

He chuckled. "No pets, then."

"I'd rather have a home full of children."

"And when's that going to happen?" He kept his hands behind his head.

"Not sure. It won't be for a while."

"Why?"

"It'd be pretty strange if Diesel and I got engaged that quickly. People would constantly question us."

"True. But why do you care?"

I cared for a lot of reasons. "As the richest woman in the world, I'm fighting for the respect of women everywhere. It's not just about me, Thorn. I did what I had to do to keep Diesel in my life. That was different."

"So...you guys are on hold?"

"I wouldn't say that. He pretty much lives with me. We're together all the time. Maybe in a few months we can talk about it."

"Are you going to change your name?"

"Nope."

He grinned. "I have a feeling Diesel isn't going to let that slide…"

"He knows he's not a match for me."

Jessica spoke through the line. "Titan, I've got Vincent Hunt on the line."

"Thanks, Jessica," I answered. "Put him through." I hit the button when the light turned on and spoke into the speaker. "Hello, Vincent. Thorn and I are talking in my office, and you're currently on speakerphone."

Vincent's deep voice filled the space. "Hello, Thorn."

"What's up?" Thorn said casually.

"Titan, I spoke to Bruce Carol," Vincent said calmly. "Is this a good time to discuss it? Or would you rather call me back?"

Vincent agreed to investigate Bruce Carol, but I had no idea when he was doing it. "No, we can talk now." I didn't have anything to hide from Thorn. "What happened?"

Thorn moved his hands to his lap and leaned forward.

"We met for drinks," Vincent said. "I told him I wanted his advice on some business opportunities. We talked about that for a while. He didn't mention

Diesel, so it seemed like he didn't know we were on speaking terms again. I told him I made an offer to you, but you rejected it and turned Kyle Livingston against me."

I kept my poise, but my heart was beating fast. "What did he say?"

"He said some things I won't repeat," Vincent said simply.

"She can handle it," Thorn said. "Trust me."

"It doesn't matter what he said," Vincent said. "We talked a little more about it, and I said I wasn't a big fan of yours. He didn't add anything else to it. The conversation died away, and we said our good-byes. He thinks I'm going to call him for a bigger discussion about my business plans, but I'll never make the call."

I exchanged a look with Thorn, seeing the pissed look on his face. He didn't take Bruce's insults as well as I did.

Vincent continued. "It's safe to say he hates you. Has no respect for you. Doesn't think highly of women in general. I'm not sure if I can assume he's the one behind those attacks on your reputation, but if it's going to be anyone, it's probably him. That's what I gathered."

"Thanks for trying, Vincent," I said.

"When Diesel and Titan confronted him," Thorn said. "He denied everything. You think he's telling the truth?"

"I wasn't there," Vincent said. "But I don't see the benefit of him admitting the truth. He did impersonate Diesel, and that's a federal offense. He's a sleazebag, so I wouldn't put it past him to lie to your face despite the thrill he would get out of it."

Thorn and I exchanged another look.

"If I find out anything else, I'll let you know," Vincent said.

"Thank you." I wrapped up the conversation then hung up. "What do you think?"

"It's probably him," Thorn said. "He seems like the most obvious suspect."

I was glad he didn't think it was Diesel anymore. "I guess I'll have to keep an eye out for him."

"I doubt he's a threat to you. The only skeleton in your closet is Diesel, and that's out in the open. He has nothing left to throw at you. I'd say you just forget about him and move on."

"Yeah, you're probably right."

"Let him slip through the cracks and be forgotten...like he should be."

DIESEL WASN'T COMING BACK INTO TOWN UNTIL three a.m.

It was too late for us to see each other, so I went to bed.

But the hours trickled by, and I didn't get any sleep. The last three days had been long, far longer than they should have been. I missed the scruffy kisses I used to get by the door. I missed hearing the shower run at the same time every day. I missed having dinner with him every night.

I missed my man.

Despite the late time of night, I grabbed a bag and headed to his place. Instead of calling my driver, I took a cab to his building a few blocks over. The elevator took me to his floor, and I stepped inside his dark penthouse. I left one light on so he would know I was there, and I headed into his bedroom. The bed was perfectly made because the maids had been there, and I pulled on one of his t-shirts before I got into bed. The sheets didn't smell like him anymore because they'd just been washed. My phone was on the nightstand, and I lay there with my eyes closed as I waited for him to come home. The comfort got to me, and I gently slipped into sleep.

The sound of a belt hitting the floor and pants coming undone slowly pulled me from sleep. A gentle thud from a heavy bag filled the bedroom. My eyes slowly opened, and I saw Diesel standing there in his boxers. He pulled his shorts down then crawled into bed with me. "I knew you would be here." His warm body surrounded mine, and he pressed hot kisses against my skin. His lips dragged down my neck and nipped at my collarbone.

My fingers dug into his hair and I moaned in happiness, feeling my strong man surround me. "I missed you…"

"Baby, I missed you more." He gripped the back of my thong and dragged it down my body before he moved between my legs. He pressed me into the mattress before he slid his cock into me, slowly pushing inside until he was completely sheathed.

"Diesel…" My ankles locked together at his lower back, and I pulled him deeper into me, loving the way he felt inside me. It was identical to every other time we made love, but it never stopped feeling brand new. My hands never stopped shaking, and my heart never rested. I wasn't Tatum Titan with this man. I was just a woman madly and deeply in love.

He rocked into me slowly, his face pressed close to mine. "Fuck…you did miss me."

My pussy was soaking wet, my body ready for him the second he walked through the door. His perfect body and handsome face didn't just make me melt. It was his strong heart, the love in his eyes, and the connection between our two souls. My nails clawed down his back. He made love to me on the very bed where he'd fucked all the others of his past, but now my love had erased them. There was only me, the only woman who'd ever mattered to him.

"Come for me." He breathed into my mouth. "You're so beautiful right now I'm not going to last." He folded my legs farther and tilted my hips deeper, intensifying the angle and rubbing his body against my clit.

My hands gripped his ass, and I yanked him harder into me, my nails testing the skin of his tight ass. I could feel how hard he was inside me, feel the way he thickened to a new level. He refrained from taking the plunge for me, but he wouldn't be able to hold on forever. Knowing I could make this experienced man climax so quickly flattered me, because that meant he wanted me just as much as I wanted him. "Almost there..."

He pounded into me harder, giving me deep strokes that hit the perfect spot every time.

My hands moved to his flexed biceps, and I held on tightly as the orgasm rocked through my system. Powerful and blinding, it shot through me like a lightning bolt. My body tightened everywhere, not just my pussy around his cock. I sucked in a deep breath before I let out a moan, coming all around him. "Yes..."

"Fuck." He gave me a few more pumps before he released deep inside me, filling my tight pussy with his load. Sheathed to the base, he stayed idle as he finished, mounds of his come sitting inside me.

I finally caught my breath, satisfied after three lonely nights without him. My fingers dug into his hair, and I fisted the strands I could recognize by touch. I looked into his handsome face, seeing the sex-crazed expression in his eyes. He was satisfied too, but he also wanted more, just as I did.

His cock slowly softened inside me, but he didn't pull out. He stayed buried between my legs like he didn't want to leave. The clean sheets were now soaked with sex, soaked with me. I marked his territory, had claimed his bed. This man was all mine, and I wasn't going to share him with anyone—ever.

He pressed his forehead to mine before he kissed the corner of my mouth.

My thighs squeezed his waist, and I kept him tightly against me. "Stay."

He kissed my jawline until his mouth reached my ear. "I'll stay forever."

My hands explored his back, feeling the powerful muscles of his body and his soft skin. I clung to him, latched on so he couldn't escape. I writhed even though the climax had long passed. I wanted more of him, but there was nothing left to take. I adored this man with every fiber of my soul. "I love you." I spoke into his ear, my lips barely touching the shell of his ear.

He turned his face back to me, his intense eyes reserved just for me. "I love you too, baby."

My hand cupped his cheek, and I felt the stubble of his face with my thumb. It was rough and masculine, just the way I liked it. Diesel was a beautiful man, but one who was rugged and manly too. His cologne was testosterone, and his deodorant was sex appeal. He was all man, head to toe. He was exactly what I wanted in another person, someone was who strong enough for me. I'd fallen in love with him for many reasons, not just because he was unbelievable in bed, but because he was unbelievable in every other aspect. "Marry me..."

He held my gaze, but his expression slowly started to change. Instead of looking surprised or shaken, his gaze held the same intensity. His hand slowly slid to my waist, his thumb resting on my belly and his fingertips against my rips just under-neath my tits.

The words were just as surprising to me. I hadn't been planning on saying them. Just the other day, I'd told Thorn I wasn't going to marry Diesel for a while. But all pragmatism went out the window when I looked into his gorgeous eyes. I saw the only man who could make me so weak, the only one who could make me so strong. There was no other man I would love this way, no man I would ever love more. Our short separation made me a little crazy, made me love him even harder than I did before. I didn't want to be apart. All I wanted was to be closer, to be together even more. "I don't care if it's too soon. I don't care what anyone thinks. I want you to be my husband, and I want us to be happy."

His hand moved farther up, his thumb resting on my sternum while his fingers surrounded my tit. He was feeling the vibrations of my heartbeat, feeling the way my body responded to him. "I'm supposed to ask you, baby."

"Doesn't matter who asks whom," I whispered.

"You don't have a ring."

"I don't need a ring. You know I'm not the kind of woman who needs a proposal. I'm not the kind of

woman who needs diamonds. All I need is you
—just you."

Still buried inside me, he looked down into my
face. His eyes were difficult to read because he hid
his emotions from me. "No."

My hands moved up his chest, but they stopped
when I heard his answer. "No?"

"No," he repeated. "I want to ask you, Titan."

My fingers dug into his chest as I felt the disappointment sweep through me.

"I want to tell you I love you. I want to give you a
ring. I want it to be a surprise."

I didn't want to wait. I'd just poured my heart out
to this man, and I didn't want to walk away feeling
like a fool. I knew he loved me; there was no doubt
of that. But he wanted to do this on his terms. I
couldn't rush him if he didn't want to be rushed.
"Okay." I had been carried away by my spontaneity.
My passion destroyed my objectivity. I lost my mind
in the clouds of lust and love.

He shifted his weight and leaned over the bed to
the nightstand. He opened the drawer, grabbed
something, and then came back to me. Between his
forefinger and thumb was a white gold band with a
small diamond in the center.

I immediately tensed, holding my breath and flinching.

"Titan, will you marry me?" He wore a smile as he looked down at me, still holding the ring for me to see.

"Diesel..."

Without waiting for an answer, he slipped the ring onto my left hand. It was a perfect fit.

I held up my hand so I could look at it. The diamond was small, but its clarity was hypnotizing. It was simple, just like me. It would accentuate my features and match my personality. It matched my relationship with Diesel, simple but beautiful. "I love it..."

"It was my mother's."

My eyes shifted back to him, the emotion burning in my eyes. "What...?"

"My dad gave it to me a few weeks ago. Said he wanted me to give it to you."

Now I looked at the ring with new eyes. Diesel's mother wore this for decades. Vincent had picked out the perfect ring for her and vowed to love her forever. Now he'd transferred that love to his son, so he could love someone the same way. It was a great honor, a welcoming into the Hunt family that I never expected. "I don't know what to say..."

"Yes, you do," he whispered. "You just demanded me to marry you. I know you're a proud woman and won't take my rejection lightly, but don't be stubborn. Just say yes. Be my wife."

I pressed my hand against his chest, seeing the way the diamond still sparkled in the minimal light. My passion had driven us to this moment, and now I wore a diamond ring on my finger. The man I loved stared down at me, still waiting for the answer he knew was coming. I was already his. The second I put that ring on, I become his in a whole new way. I'd fallen in love with the ring at first sight, and I loved it just as much as the man who gave it to me. "Yes."

He moved his hand into my hair, and he smiled down at me before he kissed me. His cock was still inside me, and it quickly hardened into a rock-hard shaft. His kiss was gentle and loving, his heartbeat steady in our embrace. "That wasn't how I was going to ask you, but I liked it more anyway."

"And I was still surprised."

He rubbed his nose against mine. "You want to keep it a secret for a while? Until we figure out what to do?"

The second I said yes to Diesel, he became the most important person in my life. I didn't give a damn what people said about me. If they said it was too fast, that was their opinion. He was the love of my life, and I wasn't going to waste another moment pretending he was anything except exactly what he was. "No. I'll never take this off as long as I live."

13

HUNT

I COULDN'T WIPE the stupid grin off my face.

Tatum Titan was my fiancée.

She asked me. I asked her. It didn't really matter who asked whom. Now she wore my ring, and she promised she would never take it off. She wanted to spend her life with me, share everything she had with me. She wanted to be pregnant with my children, to give me boys that would grow into men and girls that would grow into queens.

I was a lucky bastard.

My father and I weren't on the best terms just yet, but I'd agreed to give our relationship a chance. So I called him and told him the good news.

He picked up instantly, hardly waiting for a ring to pass. "Hey, Diesel. How was California?"

"Boring."

"That's too bad. Did you at least golf?"

I didn't give a shit about golf. "I asked her to marry me. She said yes." California, golf, real estate...it was just a bunch of shit that didn't matter. The only person that actually mattered was going to be my wife.

My father's smile was huge through the phone. "I'm happy to hear that. I was hoping you wouldn't drag your feet."

I didn't have a chance to drag my feet. Titan didn't even ask me to marry her, she just told me to. My big dick was buried inside her, and I'd just made love to her in a way I never did with anyone else. There was never really a choice. She wanted me, and she wanted to take me.

Fucking sexy.

"She loved the ring."

My father paused for a while. "I'm glad. Your mother loved it too."

"She told me she would never take it off."

"And neither did your mother. I wish Titan could have met her. They would have hit it off."

"Yeah, I'm sure they would have."

"Any details on the wedding?"

"No," I said with a chuckle. "We haven't even gotten there. I'm not sure what she wants to do.

Knowing her, probably something quick and simple, which is fine by me. But we aren't skipping the honeymoon…"

It was the first time I'd heard my dad chuckle in years. "I see where your head is at."

If only he knew what position I was in when I asked her to marry me.

"Thank you for letting me know. I know the two of you will have a long and happy life together."

"Thanks, Dad. I'm sure we will." It was still strange to call him that, but it was getting easier.

My father paused again. "Maybe we could all go out to dinner to celebrate. I'll bring Jax along."

"Yeah, sure. I'll ask her."

"Let me know." He hung up.

I was just about to call Brett when I saw the article right on the front page of Google. *Tatum Titan: Engaged for a Second Time in Two Months?* They had pictures of her walking into her building sporting the ring I gave her. They had a close-up of the ring Thorn had originally given her, and they were comparing the two.

Like they were comparing my love against Thorn's.

I'd thought our secret would have lasted longer than that.

I STOPPED BY THE STUDIO AND MET WITH THE journalist who'd interviewed me the first time. Just like last time, they had no problem getting me a slot on the air. To them, this was exclusive footage every other network would kill for.

For me, it was a chance to set the record straight.

They sat me down in the same seating area as before, and after a few questions, we were on the air.

I was prepared to put every rumor to rest. I was prepared to come clean to the world, to open my heart and let everyone take a peek inside.

John faced me, his square glasses on the bridge of his nose. "There are rumors going around that you and Tatum Titan are engaged. She was spotted walking into her building this morning with a diamond ring on her finger. Are the accusations true?"

"Yes." I didn't smile as I spoke, but I felt the happiness in my chest. "They are."

John had been a journalist for decades, and even he was slightly surprised by my honesty. "Really? When did this happen?"

"I came back from a business trip from California last night. The distance made me realize I didn't want to be without her, not even for a day. So I asked her to marry me...and she said yes."

"Some people say it's a little soon. Do you agree?"

"I don't care what people think." I didn't mean to come off cold, but that was how I felt. "I've been with a lot of women in my lifetime. None has been like Titan. I've known she was the one for a long time, long before she was ever mine. She said we're soul mates, and I agree with her." I was opening up my world to strangers, but I wanted everyone to stop their obsession with our lives. If they knew everything, there would be nothing left to be intrigued by.

"She was engaged to Thorn Cutler a little over a month ago," John said. "And their relationship lasted for over a year."

I knew those statements would be thrown my way. "She has a lot of respect for Thorn and still loves him, but when she met me, neither of us could deny what was between us. What we have is stronger than love."

John nodded even though there was no way he could possibly understand.

"My father lost my mother far too early in life. He was the one who told me it wasn't too soon to marry Titan. If I knew she was the one, it would be a disgrace to our love to wait just out of principal. So I'm not going to wait. I'm going to spend my life with her."

"Does that mean you and Vincent Hunt are on speaking terms again?"

I nodded. "We're working on our relationship. He apologized for the things he's done, I've apologized for the things I've done. We both realize that family is the most important thing on this earth, and we need to put our differences aside. Our relationship isn't perfect by any means...but at least we have one."

I WAS SITTING IN THE BACK SEAT OF MY CAR AS MY driver took me to Stratosphere. I'd finished my interview, dodged a group of reporters, and now sat comfortably behind the blacked-out windows of the car.

Titan called.

I pressed the phone to my ear. "Hey, baby. I'm on my way to Stratosphere."

The smile in her voice reached my ear before she even spoke. "I saw your interview."

My elbow rested on the door handle, and I kept

my gaze out the window, picturing the way her ring sparkled at that very moment. It seemed pointless to explain my actions when my intentions were so obvious.

"You controlled the narrative before someone else could."

"And to brag a little."

She chuckled. "I'm the one who should be bragging, Diesel."

Instantly, the warmth flooded through my body. The fact that she thought we were equals made me adore her even more. I got to marry the strongest and most intelligent woman in the world, share my life with her, and she thought she got the better bargain. It was a little ridiculous. "Now the whole world knows. They'll probably talk about it for a day or two. Something else will come up, and they'll forget about us."

"Hopefully."

The traffic cleared up, and I was just down the street from her place. "I'll be there in five minutes."

"Then we can continue the conversation in my office."

I was excited to see the ring on her finger in public. It would be the first time she was open about her love for me inside Stratosphere. Every other time we were in that building together, it was painful professionalism. I might have to lift up her skirt and fuck her on the desk out of principal. "Alright."

I arrived minutes later and took the elevator to the top floor. I didn't have any ownership of the company anymore, but that was about to change. It didn't seem productive to buy out my share of the company again when I would own half of everything she had and she would own half of all my possessions.

I ignored the smiles from our assistants and invited myself into her office. I shut the door behind me, not caring what the girls thought. Maybe I'd fuck her. Maybe I wouldn't. They got paid either way, so it didn't matter.

I looked at Titan behind her desk, a queen without a crown. She finished writing a memo, her frame perfectly straight with her shoulders back. Her ring reflected the lights from the ceiling, casting gentle rainbows across the wall. She didn't look exhausted even though we didn't sleep last night. Her elegance was unbreakable, her poise unmatched.

She set aside her pen and rose to her feet, dropping her tasks like they weren't important. Normally, she finished whatever she was doing before she addressed me, probably because she didn't classify anything I had to say as more important than whatever she was working on. But all of that seemed to change the second she put on my ring.

She came around the desk, wearing a soft smile that was reserved only for me. Her hands reached my chest and slid over my jacket as she leaned into me and kissed me on the mouth. It wasn't simple and quick, but a sensual embrace she would give me when I walked inside her penthouse after work.

I liked the change. I liked being greeted like a lover even when we were at work. We used to sneak around and lie constantly, much to my annoyance. But now she wore her heart on her sleeve, not caring about all the eyes staring at us. Now I was the most important thing in her life—and she showed it.

My hands squeezed her small waist as I pulled her farther into me. I loved feeling the swell of her tits against my hard chest. If I pulled her tightly enough, kissed her with a little tongue, I could make her nipples press through her bra and blouse and grind against me. She was in stilettos, shoes she wore as casually as slippers, and she was a little taller than I was used to. I still had to crane my neck down to look at her, my height exceeding hers exponentially.

She rubbed her nose against mine before she pulled away, a smile still on her face.

I loved being the reason behind that smile.

"You looked handsome on TV."

"You think I always look handsome."

"True." Her hands slid down my chest before she pulled them away altogether.

"What did Thorn think?"

"I haven't talked to him yet. I didn't know you were going on national TV and telling the world..."

"I guess I should have given you a heads-up." I was too busy being romantic to think twice about it. I figured she'd told Thorn the second she walked out the door that morning.

"Did you tell your father?"

"Yes."

"And what did he say?"

"That he wants to have dinner tonight to celebrate."

"That's nice."

"And he's going to bring Jax."

Her eyes lit up. "Your brother?"

"Yeah."

"I'm excited to meet another Hunt. The other two I met are pretty great."

"But not as great as I am." My arm moved around

her waist even though she just stepped away from me.

"Of course not." Like she couldn't keep her hands off me, she returned her hand to my chest. "I should get back to work. If I keep touching you like this, nothing is going to get done..."

"Would that be the worst thing in the world?"

Her eyes shifted back and forth as she looked into mine. "No, it wouldn't. And that's the problem." She kissed the corner of my mouth before she stepped away. "I guess we'll see what kind of headlines roll in..."

"And ignore them."

She sat down in her chair, the same smile on her lips. "Sounds like a good idea to me. Did you want to get caught up with Stratosphere? I figured there was no point in getting our lawyers involved."

"I don't think so either." A year ago, if someone had told me I was going to marry the richest woman in the world, I wouldn't have believed them. And then I would have cared about how it benefited me in the hierarchy or wealth. With her wealth combined with mine, I would be the richest man in the world. It was a goal I'd always wanted to attain, but I'd never thought it was possible. But the biggest surprise of all hit me next.

I didn't care.

It didn't matter how much money was in my bank account. My most valuable asset was right in front of me. She brought me joy that couldn't be bought. She made me smile just by walking into the room. All the women I'd bedded before her were erased from my memory because they never happened.

She was the only one.

I took a seat, and we got to work.

Not five minutes later, one of the girls spoke through the intercom. "Titan, Thorn is here to see you."

Titan didn't hesitate before she answered. "Send him in."

Thorn walked inside in slacks and a collared shirt. He'd ditched the jacket and tie that afternoon, obviously spending his day with a more casual air. He obviously hadn't been expecting to see me there because he nearly did a double take when he saw me. "I'm guessing the news is actually right this time?"

"Yep." She held up her left hand, showing her diamond ring. Despite the way Thorn and she had parted ways, I knew he would be happy for her. He'd always been a great friend to her, no matter what.

Thorn walked around the desk, his hands in his pockets. He let out a low whistle. "That's a nice diamond." He took her hand and examined it closer. The diamond was significantly smaller than the one he'd bought for her, which had probably cost him millions. Mine was a fraction of the price, but that didn't dilute its value. "It suits you." He dropped her hand and gave her a smile. "I guess I thought the story was bogus because I saw it on the news before you told me." Even though he kept his expression friendly, his tone was accusatory.

"I didn't tell her before I did it." I didn't want Titan to take the heat for something I did. "And then I came over here directly afterward to talk about it. She didn't have any time."

Thorn's eyes shifted to me for a moment before he turned back to her. "Well, in that case, congratulations." He extended his arms.

She moved into his embrace and hugged him tightly. Her smile was gone, but a much deeper reaction took place. The approval of this man meant everything to her, like he really was a brother to her.

It would be easy for me to get jealous, now that she was officially my fiancée. I could get more possessive, more irrational, more territorial, and I probably would, but it was unnecessary to feel that way toward Thorn. If anything, I should be even more grateful for him. He was family to her, so he would be family to me too.

Thorn pulled away first. "Diesel did a good job picking that out."

"It was his mother's," Titan said quietly as she glanced at her ring again.

Thorn turned back to me, a meaningful expression on his face. His features were as hard as usual, but there was a distinct softness too. He turned back to her before he gave a slight nod. "That's nice."

"It is." She lowered her hand again, but her thumb rubbed the band. She couldn't stop touching it, treasuring it. She didn't do that with her first ring. Whenever she was home, she never wore it.

"So, does that mean I'm the best woman or whatever?" Thorn asked.

"Actually, I was going to have you give me away," Titan said. "If you agree."

Thorn's expression completely softened, sharing an expression he only showed her behind closed doors. I'd never witnessed it before because I'd never been a member of his inner circle. But now he didn't care if I saw his vulnerability, his heart on his sleeve. He gave her a heartfelt expression, becoming more than just a hard man. His throat shifted slightly when he swallowed. His gaze darted away quickly before he held her expression again. "I'd be honored, Tatum."

Titan's eyes gently built up with tears, but before Thorn could notice, she blinked quickly and reabsorbed the moisture. Crying wasn't a habit for her. She considered it a sign of weakness rather than a natural emotion.

"Does that mean there will be a wedding?" Thorn asked.

I spoke because Titan seemed overwhelmed. "We haven't talked about it yet. But I'm sure it'll be something small, something private." Titan knew a lot of people, but I couldn't picture her wanting them all to witness the happiest day of her life. She was fiercely protective of her privacy. I didn't want anyone there either, except a few people. A big party seemed pointless to me. It was about the two of us, not hundreds of eyes staring at us.

Titan had enough time to swallow her emotion altogether, hiding it like it had never happened in the first place. Thorn didn't seem to notice, and that was the difference between the two of us. I knew her well enough to spot the subtle changes in her mood. He didn't pay nearly as much attention. "Vincent wants to get together for dinner tonight. Diesel's other brother is going to be there too."

"That sounds nice." Thorn slid his hands into his pockets.

"I'll let you know when and where." She crossed her arms over her chest, her brilliant ring still noticeable.

Thorn cocked an eyebrow. "I thought this was a family thing."

She cocked her eyebrow in return, a slight smile on her face. "And you're family, Thorn."

BRETT WAS ALREADY THERE WHEN I TOOK A SEAT IN the booth. Anytime we met for lunch, it was always at the same sports bar we'd been going to for years. Instead of having a nice lunch, we preferred to fill our stomachs with beer. He grinned at me, knowing exactly why I'd asked him to meet before I even said anything. "Congratulations." A beer was already sitting in front of me, so he clinked his glass against mine. "Took you long enough though."

I was too happy to care about the insult he just gave me. I took a drink from the glass before I set it down again. "I meant to tell you, but everything happened so fast."

"It's okay," he said. "I heard everything from your lips—on TV."

I rolled my eyes.

"What was that about anyway?"

"I knew the rumors and headlines would be worse than the truth, so I decided to take control of the narrative. There's nothing left to be intrigued by if everything is out in the open. I just want people to accept Titan and me so we can move on with our lives and be happy."

"Titan doesn't seem like the kind of woman who cares what people think."

She cared when it affected the people she loved. "She does care...a little."

Brett drank from his glass, and we shared a moment of comfortable silence. My brother and I had always been close, and we shared the kind of intimacy that was innately real. Sometimes we didn't need to say anything to each other, but we still enjoyed each other's company. I had a similar relationship with Pine and Mike, but not to the same extent. "We're getting together for dinner tonight, a small celebration. You should come."

"Who's we?" he asked.

I knew what he was really asking. "Vincent will be there. Jax will be too."

Brett's expression slowly fell, the disappointment sinking into his bones.

"You should come, Brett."

He masked his discomfort by taking a drink of his beer. "I don't know, man."

I'd never told him I'd buried the hatchet with my father. I hadn't seen him lately, and there simply wasn't time. "I told him I wanted to start over. I don't necessarily accept everything he did to both of us, but I don't hate him anymore. He seems like a different person now, as am I. The last time I saw him cry was at Mom's funeral. And when I let him back into my life...he had a few tears."

Brett's expression remained just as hard as ever, but out of principal.

"I can't tell you what to do, Brett. But I genuinely think he's sorry."

His fingers wrapped around his glass, and he stared at the amber liquid.

"And remember, Jax is your brother too. We should all see each other."

"Yeah..."

"I don't want there to be this divide between us. I want to celebrate with him and with you. I don't want to keep you guys separate for the rest of my life."

He rested his arm over the back of the booth, his eyes still on his beer.

I knew I couldn't force him to make a decision, and I couldn't force him to do what I wanted. All I could do was give him a nudge and hope he went in the right direction. "We're meeting at seven. Hope I see you there."

14

TITAN

ONE MEETING RAN MUCH LATER than I anticipated, so I was stuck in my office wrapping up other projects I hadn't had a chance to complete. Work used to be my life, but now it took second place to the man I adored. Money used to mean more to me because it represented power and independence. But now all the money in the world meant nothing in comparison to Diesel. As long as we were together, I didn't care if we were broke.

I'd rather be in bed, my fiancé's lips all over me.

My phone vibrated on the white desk, and his name appeared on the screen.

I answered immediately. "Hey."

"Hey, baby. When are you coming home?"

I liked the way he referred to my penthouse as home. We hadn't decided where we would live, but that didn't seem to matter. Whether it was his place or mine, it would feel right. "I got caught up at the office, unfortunately."

He didn't give me a hard time about it, knowing exactly how dedicated I was. "I just got out of the shower, and I was about to head out. You want to meet at the restaurant?"

"That's fine." I would stop by my place and change, but that would only take a few minutes. "I'll see you in about thirty minutes or so. Is Brett coming?"

Diesel gave a long pause before he answered. "I doubt it. We talked about it at lunch today, but he didn't seem thrilled by the idea. Said he would think about it."

It was a complicated situation, and I knew it couldn't be rushed. "I hope he'll be there."

His masculine voice was full of sorrow. "Yeah...me too."

Another pause ensued, but it only happened because we wanted to be on the phone together a little longer. We would see each other in less than an hour, but it seemed like a lifetime. I missed this man whenever we weren't together, even if that break only lasted a few hours.

He spoke first. "I can't wait to see you."

"Me too."

"Love you."

Now he said it every time he got off the phone, and he was always the first one to say it. It'd become a routine between us, and I hoped that routine would never change. "I love you too."

We hung up and I got back to work, speeding up because I wanted to get out of there as quickly as possible. I didn't stay late at the office very often anymore, usually because I wasn't as motivated. But if I didn't take care of these orders, it would haunt me tomorrow.

My phone rang again. This time, it was Vincent.

I put him on speakerphone so I could keep working. "Hey, Vincent."

His tone was lighter than Diesel's, but his words contained the same intensity that seemed to be shared among the Hunt men. "You know, I'm not going to be able to call you Titan much longer." There was a hint of happiness in his voice. I hadn't spoken to him about the news yet. It had just happened last night, so I really hadn't had the chance to talk to anyone about it.

"You can call me Tatum." I wasn't planning on changing my last name, but it would be strange for my father-in-law to refer to me by my maiden name.

"Beautiful name."

"Thanks."

He paused over the line, drawing out the silence just as he would if we were sitting in my office. Diesel must have gotten that from his father without even realizing it. "My son couldn't have chosen a better woman to spend his life with. My wife would be thrilled, and I'm very thrilled."

I hadn't been expecting an emotional conversation, but anytime his late wife was mentioned, I was overcome with emotion. I never knew my mother. Did she ever have regrets about what she did? Would she be proud of me? What if Diesel's mother were still around? Would she be the mother I never had? She sounded incredible. "Thank you, Vincent. But I consider myself to be the lucky one. Your son is a wonderful man. I know he'll spend his life making me happy."

"I have no doubt of that either. I can't take all the credit for his character, but I'm proud of who he is nonetheless. And I'm proud of his good taste. When I say he couldn't have chosen anyone better, I truly mean that."

Vincent had slowly wormed his way into my heart, and now I didn't just see him as Diesel's father. I saw him as something much more, a shadow of my own father. He made me feel the way my own father did, that I was special—that I was loved. I hadn't felt that way in a long time. "Thank you..."

"I'll see you tonight. Jax is looking forward to meeting you."

"I'm looking forward to it too."

"And Tatum?"

"Yes?"

"You wear that ring well."

I STEPPED INTO MY PENTHOUSE AND IMMEDIATELY raided my closet. The black dress I had on was nice, but it was too stiff for a fun evening out. I pulled out a tight purple dress with matching pumps along with a diamond necklace. I quickly changed my wardrobe then touched up my makeup in the bath-room. Anytime I looked in the mirror, the brilliance of the ring always distracted me.

I had been able to afford to buy my own jewelry for nearly a decade. Anytime I wanted something beautiful, I could buy it myself. I never needed a man for anything, and I prided myself for that. But Diesel's diamond meant more to me than anything else I could buy—because it was priceless.

I was about to walk out the door when Thorn called me.

"Hey, I'm about to leave right now," I said as I grabbed my clutch from the dresser.

"Want me to pick you up?"

"My driver is out front. Besides, I'm closer anyway."

"Alright. I'll see you soon."

"Bye." I hung up and got into the elevator. After I hit the button, it slowly sank to the bottom floor. The ring felt heavy on my left hand, the weight noticeable on my slender finger. My neck was always decorated with diamonds, as was my wrist. But I rarely wore rings because it didn't seem natural. The weight distracted me when I typed, and when I handled a pen, the metal band always tapped against the metal.

But now I couldn't picture myself without the ring. It was already a part of me.

It was all of me.

The doors opened, and I walked across the empty lobby. It was decorated luxuriously, with fine couches and tables, a coffee station, and the large boxes where tenants received their mail. The glass door opened as a man walked inside, and after a few steps, he looked up to meet my gaze.

I'd recognize him anymore.

Bruce Carol looked me right in the eye, silent hostility written all over his expression. In a thick black coat with black gloves, he looked like a man who had just walked through a storm. I felt ice-cold the second he looked at me, feeling dread form in the pit of my stomach. Instinct kicked in, and a spike of adrenaline circulated in my blood. Terror gripped my heart.

A warning screamed in my mind.

He pulled his hand out of his pocket, and in his grasp was a black gun. He raised it and pointed directly at my chest.

I halted, my heels no longer tapping against the tile floor. There wasn't time to feel afraid, not when death was looking at me right in the face. All I could think about was survival, how I would get out of this lethal situation. The doorman outside the building was facing the opposite way. There was no one else in the space. The elevators weren't lit up because no one was descending to the lobby.

It was only him and me.

He took another step toward me, pointing the gun right at my face.

Now wasn't the time to be stubborn, but I refused to raise my hands in the air. I refused to let my fear appear on my face. I refused to do anything but stare at him with the same ferocity. "If you can only beat me with a gun, then you'll never win."

His blue eyes didn't blink as they remained trained on me. His hand didn't shake as he aimed the barrel right at my heart. My words didn't seem to leave a mark. It was like he hadn't heard them at all.

I didn't have any way of defending myself. There wasn't a table nearby, even a lamp. All I had was the clutch in my hand. I could throw it as his face, but he would fire first. All I had were my words. There were cameras in the corners of the lobby, but I suspected no one was watching because someone would have been down here by now. "You still have your children. If you do this, you'll lose them too."

"I lost them because of you." His finger moved over the trigger.

I wasn't ashamed to admit I was afraid, but if this was how I lost my life, I would maintain as much dignity as I could. I wouldn't give him the satisfaction of begging or apologizing. I would give him absolutely nothing until I gave my last breath.

And my last thought would be of Diesel.

The silence intensified. I could hear my breathing, and I could hear his too. I waited for something to happen, for someone to walk through the doors and disrupt the nightmare. I waited for him to lower the gun and come to his senses. "Money doesn't mean anything. You have so much more to live for."

"Money doesn't mean anything to you because you have it." He stepped forward farther. "But now you won't."

And then he shot me.

It was painless.

All I felt was the jolt of momentum as my body was flung to the floor. I collapsed onto the tile, hitting the back of my head hard. The ground was cold, but my blood warmed the surface of my skin as it dripped everywhere.

My heart beat faster, compensating for the lack of blood.

I immediately felt weak with shock.

I stared at the fluorescent lights up above, my beautiful dress ruined with my own death. My clutch had fallen to the ground at some point. Life was fading from my eyes, and Diesel came into my mind. He wouldn't survive without me. He would never know happiness again. I had to survive, but I didn't know how.

Bruce stepped over me, the gun pointed down at me. It was aimed right at my face, the black barrel still smoking from the previous bullet. His rage hadn't been satisfied with the first shot. He obviously needed more to complete his vendetta.

He wanted to finish me off, destroy my face so I wouldn't even have an open coffin funeral. He couldn't handle the way I'd gracefully destroyed him, the way Diesel sided with me in making our deal. Bruce was a sexist pig that only knew how to play dirty. He solved this problem with the same disgust he handled all of his issues.

I couldn't let that happen.

His finger moved over the trigger.

The second I moved, I would rush my speed of death. But I'd rather die bleeding out all over the floor than let this bastard shoot me in the face. And I'd rather die with his cold body beside me, so Diesel wouldn't have to suffer through the trial that would drag out for years on end.

I'd rather take Bruce with me.

Before he could pull the trigger, I kicked him in the knee and knocked his hand out of the way at the same time.

The gun went off, shooting the elevator door.

I kicked him again even though I was bleeding even more. My life was draining away; I was getting weaker by the second. I only had minutes left, maybe not even that.

Bruce stumbled forward and dropped the gun.

I snatched it, cocked it, and pointed it right at his face. "Looks like I win again." I pulled the trigger.

Bang.

He fell to the floor, his body immediately idle.

I pointed the gun at him again, aiming for his neck.

I shot him again. Bang.

With the gun still hot, I set it on the tile beside me. Then I lay there, feeling the darkness cover me. Dying was exactly the same was falling asleep. All I had to do was close my eyes and wait for it to pass. The pain would end. The suffering would be over. I'd made my mark on the world, and I would still be remembered after I was gone.

I only wished I could stay.

I had more life to live.

I had a man I loved.

I didn't have my children.

Voices erupted around me, ambulance lights flashed through the windows, and then a man appeared over me. It must have been a paramedic because he shouted medical terminology. I was placed on a gurney and then rolled toward the ambulance.

I couldn't hold on any longer.

I looked at the man above me, a paramedic in his forties. "Do you know who I am?"

"Yes. We're getting you to the hospital, Ms. Titan." He was professionally calm despite the blood dripping across the sidewalk and road.

"Do something for me."

He helped the men place me in the back of the ambulance. The wheels were locked, the doors were shut, and then we were speeding through New York City. "If I can, I will."

I was slipping away. I couldn't feel my hands anymore. The sensation in my legs had disappeared a long time ago. I could barely feel my engagement ring on my finger. "Tell Diesel Hunt I love him."

15

HUNT

I WAS the first one there, and Thorn arrived a moment later.

Thorn walked up to me and shook my hand. "First ones here, huh?"

"Yep. Titan had to work late tonight."

"Yeah, I called her on the way over here. She should be here any minute. She was walking out when I called her."

"Good." I didn't want to wait longer than I had to. I wanted to stare at her beautiful face, kiss her on the lips, and wrap my arm around her waist. I wanted to pull her close to me, to tell the world that this former playboy had settled down for the right woman—and I wouldn't have settled for anyone else. "I miss her."

He rolled his eyes. "Don't make me throw up, alright?"

I smiled. "I'll try."

"So, Jax, huh?"

"Yeah." I wasn't sure what I would say to my brother. It'd been a long decade of silence. The last time I'd spoken to him, he'd warned me about our father. He obviously still had some kind of connection to me.

"I've never met him." He moved his hands into his pockets. "I hope he's more like Brett than he is like Vincent."

"Vincent's not so bad…" I found myself defending my father when I would normally tear him down. It had become apparent how similar we were throughout the past few months. From our appearance to our mannerisms to our opinions, we were a lot alike. I just hoped I could learn from his mistakes before I made them myself.

Thorn nodded. "I'm glad you guys made up. I knew it was important to Titan that you reconnect."

"Yeah, she knows what's best for me."

"Then, good thing you're marrying her," he teased. "Because you're going to be getting a lot more than that."

I thought of our past, of everything we've been

through. "I don't mind having her boss me around from time to time..."

Thorn must have known my true meaning because he grinned. "TMI, man."

My father strode through the door with Jax by his side. He located us a moment later, and they walked across the restaurant as they headed our way.

Jax was exactly as I remembered him, built and strong. He wore jeans and a long-sleeved shirt, olive green with a slim fit. He had the same eyes I did, and his resemblance to our father was striking. It was obvious to anyone who met us that we were brothers. Brett and I had a lot of similarities, but people could mistake Jax and me for twins.

My father stopped in front of me and didn't extend his hand. This time, he wrapped his arms around me and gave me a hug.

I hugged him back.

He patted me on the back as he pulled away, staring at me with happiness in his eyes. He didn't smile, but he didn't need to. The joy was in his eyes, just the way it was whenever he used to look at my mother.

He turned to Thorn next and shook his hand. "Nice to see you, Thorn."

"You too, Vincent," Thorn responded.

Vincent stepped away then turned to Jax. "I'm sorry that I've kept the two of you apart for so long. It shouldn't have happened. I can't erase the past, but maybe we can make up for lost time."

Looking at Jax wasn't full of bitterness the way it was with my father. I didn't have a single negative feeling toward him. It was a difficult situation, and I didn't judge him for siding with my father. There was no clear answer, and he'd never personally done anything to me. I still saw him as my brother—and that would never change. "How about we skip the handshake and just do the hug?" It was a cheesy icebreaker, but it was better than nothing.

He gave me a smile that was similar to mine. "That's fine—just this once."

I hugged him and hugged me back. The embrace lasted longer than it normally would, probably longer than any other hug we'd shared. We pulled away, stepped back from each other as brothers again. "We'll have to catch up."

"Yeah," Jax said. "You bagged Tatum Titan as a wife. Pretty impressive."

"I didn't bag her. I won her." I was the only man worthy of her. No one else could match her strength, intelligence, and power.

"Whatever," Jax said with a chuckle. "That's a story I want to hear about."

"And I'll tell you when she gets here." I glanced at the door, expecting to see her walk inside. I imagined the love in her eyes when she looked at me, the way she wore her ring with immense pride.

I didn't see Titan, but I saw someone else.

Brett.

He glanced around the room before he located us in the corner. He walked toward us in a black blazer and black jeans. He held himself with confidence even though he wasn't excited for this dinner.

My father turned to him, a slight smile stretching on his face.

Brett joined us, his eyes moving to Jax. "How's it going, man?"

Jax shook his head. "A lot better now that you're here. Your cars are awesome. Sweetest ride I've had."

"Thanks." Brett turned to my father next. "Is it cool if I join you?"

My father wrapped his arm around Brett's shoulders, showing more affection than I'd ever seen him extend in his life. "It wouldn't be the same without you."

When I turned to look at Thorn, his face was pressed to his phone. It didn't seem like he was reading an email or checking his stocks, because his face was pale as snow. His hand shook slightly, and his eyes were snapped wide open. "Everything alright, man?"

He ran his hand through his hair then stumbled back like he'd tripped over something. He dragged his hand down his face, and his chest was rising and falling at a formidable rate. His breath was loud, his terror obvious.

"Thorn?" I grabbed his arm, helping him balance himself because he suddenly appeared weak.

It took him a second to overcome the shock. He still hadn't blinked yet, and his hand shook like he could barely keep his grasp on his phone. He finally put the phone in my hand, releasing a loud breath as if it took the last of his energy just to make the transfer.

Whatever left Thorn speechless must have been terrible. He wasn't the kind of guy that scared easily. I could only assume the worst, that the United States had declared war or someone had died.

I looked at the screen.

Tatum Titan in Critical Care after Being Gunned Down by Bruce Carol.

My hand shook just the way his did, but I didn't

have the strength he possessed. The phone slipped from my hand and fell to the hardwood floor, clattering loudly as the screen cracked right down the middle.

Now I couldn't breathe.

I couldn't digest the words I'd just read.

Like I was living in a nightmare, everything moved so slowly. I expected to wake up, to tell myself it was just a dream.

But it was real.

My nightmare was real.